MW01275325

Canadian Historical Mysteries – British Columbia

Jay Lang

Print ISBNs
Amazon Print 9780228625070
BWL Print 9780228625087
Ingram Print 9780228625094
B&N Print 9780228625100

BWL Publishing Inc.

Books we love to write ...
Authors around the world.

http://bwlpublishing.ca

Canadian Historical Mysteries

Rum Bullets and Cod Fish - Nova Scotia

Sleuthing the Klondike – Yukon

Who Buried Sarah- New Brunswick

The Flying Dutchman – British Columbia

Bad Omen - Nunavut

Spectral Evidence – Newfoundland

The Seance Murders – Saskatchewan

The Canoe Brigade – Quebec

Discarded – Manitoba

Twice Hung - Prince Edward Island

Jessie James' Gold – Ontario

A Killer Whisky – Alberta

Table of Contents

Dedication

To the Lyster Clan, and to all the many minds and voices who helped with my research for this novel. Also, I'd like to thank Union Bay Historical Society (Linda McKay), The Comox Museum, The Courtenay Library, The Cumberland Library and Museum, and The Nanaimo Museum. Thank you all for your invaluable information.

Acknowledgement

BWL Publishing Inc. acknowledges the Government of Canada and the Canada Book Fund for their financial support in creating the Canadian Historical Mysteries.

Funded by the Government of Canada

Chapter 1

The rolling grey sky mirrors the turbulent sea, making the line between the two indistinguishable. As soon as the small sailboat leaves the shelter of Vancouver Harbour and enters the immense open strait, wind attacks the modest craft and causes it to sway against the rising swells. I reach out and grasp the railing, feeling the vibrations of the old wood as it twists beneath the force of the elements.

Billy, my brother, looks back at me and winks, a feeble attempt at soothing my rapidly increasing anxiety. At twenty-four, five years my senior, Billy is far from a role model and even farther from being dependable. My mother, God rest her, passed only a month ago, relegating me to my last immediate family member.

"I've got this great opportunity to make some good money working at a mine on Vancouver Island," he said just a week ago.

"But you don't know a thing about mining," I retorted.

"You know that, and I know that, but the man that hired me doesn't. Plus, how hard can it be?"

At the time, I was working at a market in the city, barely making enough to put food on the table and nowhere near enough to afford to pay rent on my own.

"You have to come with me, little sis. You'll never afford the high cost of living in the city by yourself."

His words immediately caused my stomach to churn—I knew he was right. I had no choice but to pack a bag, say goodbye to all that was familiar to me, and follow reluctantly behind him.

Mother used to say that he was the spitting likeness of our father. She never explained how, but it was easy to guess what she meant. Billy never held a job past receiving the first paycheck before he was on to a new scheme to make bigger money, schemes that sometimes blurred the lines between right and wrong. The last get-rich-quick venture he embarked upon ended in his arrest and with my mother pleading at the local jail for his release. My brother committed to his story that he was completely oblivious to the fact that selling alcohol to Indigenous peoples was illegal. Seeing through Billy's web of lies, the judge sentenced him t7o six months of labour.

I wasn't as angry about his crime as I was over the strain the whole ordeal put on my mother. She was a righteous woman who fought hard throughout our childhood to instill a strong moral code in both my brother and me. And as much as she loved my brother, he was a constant source of disappointment and worry.

Although the official cause of her death was listed as heart failure, I knew that all the hard labour jobs she took on to support us, coupled with the stress my brother put on her, made her health deteriorate prematurely.

* * *

"You'd better take your sister below deck. It looks like we're going to be fighting a storm," the old captain yells to my brother.

Billy uses the railing to steady himself and make his way down the wet deck to me, then guides me to the small cabin door. "Don't worry. Everything is going to be all right. Captain Bruce knows what he's doing."

Yeah, sure he does.

I would feel a lot more confident about the captain's abilities if Billy hadn't met him in a tavern. My brother was so proud that he was able to strike a cheap passage for us to Vancouver Island. I tried to explain to him that if Captain Bruce were a reputable mariner, he wouldn't need to lower his price, but my reasoning fell on deaf ears.

The truth is, I'm not only afraid of dying out here on this creaky old sailboat, but I'm just as fearful about what will happen to us once we reach Cumberland. No doubt Billy lied to his prospective employer and portrayed himself as an expert in the mining industry. On his first day at the mine, it will be immediately obvious that he hasn't a clue what he's doing. Then, it will only be a matter of time before he's out of a job again.

Once we're off the boat, providing we live through the crossing, I'll ask Billy exactly how much money we have. I had given him the thirteen dollars I'd saved in a tin under my bed to help pay for our trip. I pray he has enough money to sustain us for a while.

A huge wave slams into the side of the small vessel, knocking tin cups and other projectiles from the dirty galley counter. I quickly sit on the narrow bench fixed to the table and brace myself. Wave after wave hits the hull as the small boat pitches and sways. It isn't long before my stomach mimicks the motion of my surroundings. I scan the small cabin for any sign of a bucket just in case I become sick, but there's nothing other than the tin cups clanking around on the floor.

The cabin door opens, and I look up just in time to see Captain Bruce and a wave of sea spray exploding behind him. He quickly maneuvers into the cabin and slides the door shut.

His face is streaming with water, and his old wool cap is dripping on the wood floor. "How are you holding up, Green-Eyes? You look a little pale. Are ya feeling seasick?" He makes his way toward me.

"My name is Heather, and I'll be fine. I'm not really used to sailing in rough seas, is all."

The captain laughs. "All you city slickers are alike that way. A few big bumps and everyone has their heads over the sides."

I force a smile before something alarming occurs to me. If Captain Bruce is in here with me, who's steering the boat? "Where is my brother?" I hope to hell the old captain hasn't left Billy in control of the small craft.

"He's at the helm, and from the look on his face, he's enjoying every minute of it. He said he feels like a cowboy in a rodeo." He laughs.

"We are city folks, born and raised. The only knowledge my brother has about rodeos comes from reading books. And to the best of my knowledge, Billy has even less experience with boats. I think I'd feel a lot better if you were out there with him."

"Just came in to grab some tobacco chew." He grabs a small packet from the shelf behind me, opens the tightly rolled pack, then takes a big pinch of brown tobacco, stuffing it in his lip. "Gimme your hand, girl." He reaches toward me.

"Pardon? Why do you want my hand?"

"In case I lose one." He laughs. "Let me see one of your hands."

Sensing he won't take no for an answer, I slowly open my hand and show it to him.

With the finesse of a striking snake, he grabs my hand. Then, he applies pressure to the flesh between my pointer finger and thumb. At first, it hurts so much, but the more he presses, the more the queasiness in my stomach starts to ease.

He smiles. "It's a little trick I learned from my grandfather years ago. He would take me fishing with him, and when the weather turned bad, my stomach did too. He got tired of cleaning up my vomit, so he'd press on my hand, and usually, it took my mind off my stomach."

"Thank you. I can't believe that worked. I'm starting to feel a lot better."

Just then, another massive wave hits and knocks the old captain into the table. He grins. "She's an angry sea today."

"How long until we reach Union Bay?"

"It'll be a while yet. If we were traveling in a straight line, we'd be there already. It's the up and down that's delaying us."

"Maybe you should go out and take the wheel."

He laughs and heads out into the angry elements. Sitting in the rocking cabin, I focus on the cadence of the tin cups as they roll back and forth along the floor. As much as I find Captain Bruce to be blunt and lacking in social graces, after spending a few minutes alone with him, I feel a lot more confident that we'll reach Vancouver Island alive. His carefree, lackadaisical demeanor convinced me he'd successfully navigated through much rougher waters than this. And he even knew how to rid me of my uneasy stomach. That kind of knowledge could only come from an experienced seaman.

* * *

It feels like a few hours pass as I sit and stare through the small, round portholes. A few times during the journey, I want to open the door and check to see if the men are still standing on the deck and haven't been swept overboard, but I know if I look once, I'll keep doing it.

Instead, I lean against the wall, close my eyes, and force myself to focus on happy times when my mother was still alive, and the three of us would play dress up or act out silly plays in our one-bedroom apartment over the furniture store. I thought those times would never end. I took for granted that my mother would always be there and I would never feel alone.

* * *

The noise from the wooden door sliding open, followed by an icy cold blast of wind, startles me out of my sleep. Billy is standing in the doorway with an arm pressing against his chest.

"Are you hurt?" I call out.

"It's nothing." He walks in and closes the door behind him.

Only when I stand up and approach him do I notice the boat isn't rocking nearly as severly now. "Let me see." I motion to his arm.

He sighs, then slides his wet jacket off. Immediately, I see a large purple and red bruise on his elbow.

"Billy, that doesn't look good. How did you hurt yourself?"

He shrugs. "Captain Bruce was at the helm and needed to relieve himself over the side of the boat. When he let go of the wheel, it started to spin, and when I reached out to stop it, my elbow got in the way."

"Can you bend it? Do you think it could be broken?"

He shakes his head. "No, it's not broken, and yes, I can bend it. We'll spend the night in Union Bay, and I'm sure it will feel much better by morning. Anyways, I didn't come down here to talk about my arm. I came to tell you we should be docking soon, so get yourself together. I'll meet you on deck."

* * *

Billy and I push against the evening wind as we make our way up the Government Dock toward The Union Bay Inn. By the time we reach the first steps of the two-level white building, my limbs are stiff from the cold. Thankfully, my brother was kind enough to carry my two small cases and his own.

In front of us, a family of three waits at the check-in desk. I lean close to Billy and whisper, "This looks like a nice inn. Shouldn't we be staying at a more affordable place?"

He smiles. "Don't worry about it. I've got it covered."

Once the family gets their room key and walks away, Billy steps up to the counter. "I'd like two rooms, please."

Two? Is he crazy? Why is he wasting money? Whatever money he has can't add up to much, and if he's not careful with every penny, we'll go hungry in no time.

Once upstairs, Billy reads the gold-covered keys, then walks me to my room. Inside is a single bed with a metal headboard, a three-drawer wooden dresser with a mirror on top, and a chair beside a large window. Billy sets my bags on the bed and turns to walk out of the room.

"Wait a second!" I prompt him to stop and turn to me. "Billy, why didn't you just get one room with two beds? I'm sure it would've been a lot cheaper."

He sighs and, for a moment, looks annoyed. "Look, Heather. I had a mother who told me what to do, and she's gone now. I don't want or need you to take her place. I'm your big brother, and you'll just have to trust that I will take care of you...of us. I'll be next door if you need me."

He has that look in his eyes, the look that says nobody can reason with him. I sit on the bed and fold my arms in front of me. "Can I at least ask you how much money we have left?"

"We have enough," he says before turning and leaving the room.

As soon as the door closes and I'm alone, I immediately miss the familiar surroundings of home. I haven't had much experience outside my old neighborhood back in Vancouver. Mom, Billy, and I have lived in the same apartment for as long as I can remember. Even the neighborhood didn't change much while I was growing up. I took a lot of comfort in knowing everyone around me, unlike Billy, who seems to have a constant itch to see new places and have new experiences. He could never sit still for too long. I think that's why he gets into trouble. He's never content.

I hear a key open the door to the next room. At least Billy will be close by. I walk to the window to look over the bay, but it's too dark to see anything.

My stomach grumbles, and I remember the last time I ate anything was this morning before we set out on our journey. I could disturb Billy to find me something to eat, but I'm more tired than hungry. Instead, I change out of my clothes and slide my nightdress over my head, then go to bed.

* * *

The morning sun seeps through the window and floods the room with a warm yellow glow. After washing my face, getting dressed, and tying my long auburn hair up in a tight bun, I put on my ankle boots and head next door to Billy's room.

I rap a few hard times before I hear stirring inside. A few long moments pass before he answers with disheveled hair and still wearing the same attire he wore yesterday.

I look at his clothes. "Did you sleep in those?"

"Heather, why are you waking me so early?"

"I don't think it's that early. If I were to guess, I'd say it's somewhere around nine AM."

"All right, well, give me some time. I'll get myself together, then meet you in the lobby."

Back in my room, I pack my things and make sure everything is tidy before hauling my bags downstairs.

I sit on a red high-back chair and wait for Billy as people walk through the lobby. The first thing I notice is how differently people dress here than in the city. Instead of colourful dresses with lace accents on the cuffs and collars, the women wear muted blues, browns, or blacks. Most have their hair fastened in tight buns, and I haven't seen one fancy hat. As for the men, the common colors for their slacks and blazers seems to be dark browns or blacks.

Billy finally makes his way to the lobby, looking far better than he did a half hour ago. His wavy, light brown hair is freshly combed, and he's changed into a clean pair of trousers and a matching blazer. I think he looks quite smart, which is confirmed when the young woman behind the desk looks up at him and smiles. Of all the things my brother lacks, good looks is not one of them. In Vancouver, he always had his pick of eligible ladies to date.

He approaches me. "I'm famished. You must be as well. Let's go into the restaurant and get some brunch."

We leave our bags in the corner of the lobby, then walk into a medium-sized room with nine tables topped with white linen cloths and shiny place settings.

"Can we afford to eat here?" I whisper to him.

"Don't start. Let's just sit and enjoy a meal. Plus, I have some exciting news for you."

A waiter wearing black pants and a white collared shirt directs us to a table by the window, then hands Billy a menu. Once he walks away, I ask Billy what news he has.

"Well, last night, at the tavern up the road—"

"What do you mean? Did you go out last night after we checked into our rooms?"

"Yes, Mother. I did. Do you want to hear what I have to say or not?"

I sigh. "I guess that's why you were still in your day clothes when you answered the door."

Billy had promised me before we left Vancouver that he would not drink anymore. It's when he drinks that he makes bad decisions. With our futures so uncertain, the last thing we need is him drunk and getting into trouble. The hunger pangs in my stomach quickly turn into nausea, and I no longer feel like eating.

My brother reads the worry in my expression and puts his hand on mine. "I know what you're thinking, Heather, but you needn't worry. Everything is under control. When Mom was dying, I promised her that I would watch out for you, and I meant it."

His light blue eyes stare into mine. I can always tell when he's trying to manipulate me or when he's being sincere. Right now, I can tell he means everything he's saying.

Attempting to calm myself, I breathe in deeply and slowly exhale. "But you promised me you wouldn't drink anymore."

"And I haven't broken my promise. I couldn't sleep last night, so I went to the tavern for a while. Captain Bruce was there. You can ask him if I drank."

"The captain was there?"

"He was. And he was the life of the place."

"Why is that?"

"Unbeknownst to me, he's quite a gifted bagpipe player. He played for hours while everyone stomped their feet and sang. It was a real hoot."

"Bagpipes? Really?" I smile. "The old captain is full of surprises."

The waiter returns and takes our order. Thankfully, my nausea has dissipated, and I can eat.

"So, is that the news you had to tell me?"

Billy shakes his head. "No. It gets better. You are not going to believe who I ran into last night."

"Who?"

"Our cousin Faye's husband, Charlie."

"But I thought they lived in Victoria?"

"They did. Apparently, Charlie was transferred up here to oversee the coke ovens."

"What's a coke oven?"

Billy laughs. "That was my first question, too. They are ovens in the ground that they put smaller pieces of coal into, then burn or render them down to make coke."

"What is coke used for?"

Billy shrugs. "I'm not sure. Charlie said something about it being used when manufacturing iron and steel."

"Interesting. So, is Faye here in Union Bay with Charlie?"

"She is. And they have a child now as well."

"Do they? That's great. And what a coincidence you would run into Charlie here. I think the last time I saw Faye was when we all went to the beach in Vancouver. Mom was so happy to be spending time with her family. I must've been about nine, and Faye was eleven. Faye and I built crab jails in the sand. She was a nice girl with pretty blond hair and a nice smile, though I remember her being very particular about which crab went into which jail." I laugh. "She had a clear vision of how she wanted things done."

"They live in a cabin down by the beach. Charlie insisted that we spend the night there before we travel to Cumberland."

"That's great and all, Billy. But aren't you supposed to show up for work today?"

"No. The boss said he expects me at the mining office by Monday. It's only Saturday, so we have lots of time. Plus, I think it will be good to spend time with Charlie. I can pick his brain about mining, so I'll know more about the job when we get there."

"That's actually a good idea," I agree. "As much as I hate to impose upon our cousin on such short notice, you'll stand a much better chance of not getting fired if you get educated about the job beforehand."

After we eat and Billy pays the waiter, I restrain myself from inquiring how much the meal cost. In the lobby, we gather our luggage and head out of the inn.

* * *

When we walk the narrow-rutted road to the cabin on the beach, the hem of my dress becomes covered in dirt. I stop to brush it off, Billy tells me not to fret about the grime, adding that because of the terrain and Union Bay is a working town, everyone probably has the same challenges with keeping clean.

The cabin is painted a robin's egg blue with white window frames and lace curtains. At the top of the freshly swept steps are two large planters with hand-painted designs. Faye must grow flowers in the urns when the season changes.

"It's very nice," I say. "Not at all what one would picture when you hear *cabin-on-the-beach*."

Just as we reach the top step, the door opens, and a very primped and perfect Faye smiles at us. "Welcome, cousins. Please come in."

I take off my ankle boots and set them on the mat beside the door, then urge Billy to do the same.

Faye has somehow escaped the years. Her smooth porcelain-like skin and her slim build resemble those of a doll that was displayed in the jewelry store window back home. "Excuse the mess," she says, leading us to the front room.

Billy and I look around the immaculate cabin. Everything from small doilies to ornaments is deliberately placed around the room, and as hard as I try, I can't see any sign of mess. It's hard to believe a child is living here. Every home I've visited that had children usually looked like a tornado had swept through.

Faye offers us tea and sets out a plate of freshly made biscuits. "I was sorry to hear about your mother." She sits down across from us.

"Thank you," I reply. "It's definitely been a challenging time."

She turns her attention to Billy. "Charlie said you are going to Cumberland to work in the mines."

He nods. "Yes. I've secured a job there. We'll be catching the train in the morning."

"I see. And you're going to Cumberland as well, Heather?"

I smile. "I am, yes."

"I wonder...if Billy will be working in the mine, what will you do to occupy your time?"

I shrug. "I haven't a clue. I suppose I'll do what I did back in Vancouver. Look for a job in a shop or maybe in a hotel."

Faye smiles. "Cumberland is a lot different than Vancouver, I assure you. It's a working town built to accommodate and service the miners. Shops and businesses are not bright and clean as they are in Vancouver. I think it will be a big shock for you."

"That's okay. I'll be going to support Billy. We're a team."

Just then, Charlie walks through the door.

Faye hollers, "Did you remember to remove your boots outside before coming in?"

"Yes, dear."

When he walks into the living room, Faye gets up to fix him a cup of tea. He sits down and, with a smile, welcomes us to his home, then says he's glad we took him up on his offer to stay the night. "We don't see much of family up here."

We visit for an hour until Charlie tells us he must go and supervise things at the coke ovens. He invites Billy along, telling him they can talk about the Cumberland mine on the way.

I am helping Faye tidy up from our tea break when a child's voice calls from the front bedroom.

"Eva is awake." Faye places the last of the cups in the sink. "I'll be right back."

A few moments later, Faye returns with a golden-haired little girl on her hip. As soon as they get close enough, I can see the strong resemblance between mother and child.

Eva looks at me with a bit of apprehension until I make a silly face, and she starts to laugh.

"She's beautiful. How old is she?"

"Two and a half."

With Faye busy tending to the child, I quickly do up the dishes, then decide to go for a walk on the beach.

* * *

Thankfully, the wind has died down over the past couple of hours, making my stroll to the shoreline pleasant. Sitting on a hollowed-out log just feet from the sea, I look over the pristine bay. I watch as the gulls pace the sandy shoreline, scouring for morsels of food.

There's a pretty little island to my right. Captain Bruce said it was called Denman Island when we sailed to the wharf yesterday. Off in the distance, a small boat passes by. It's so picturesque here, as if I'm watching a moving painting.

I stand and am about to walk closer to shore when a large shadow passes overhead. I look up to see the most spectacular sight—a large bald eagle as he swoops down and lands at the water's edge. Knowing the eagle is a predator, the gulls quickly scurry and take flight over the water. I sit back down so as not to frighten away the magnificent creature and watch him as he watches me with great curiosity. His pointed beak is yellow like amber, and his talons are long and sharp. I wish Billy were here to see this.

Back home in the city, I'd only seen eagles from a good distance, as the street cars and bustling roads deter them. Gulls are common, though, and often gather near park benches and scrounge around the seawalls and grassy areas where people stop to eat.

The eagle flutters his wings in the shallows, then turns his attention to deeper waters. Motionless, he stares off into the blue for a considerable amount of time. Then, as silently as he arrived, his magnificent wings open, and he takes flight. I stand to get a better view as the eagle glides effortlessly over the sea and, with stealth-like precision, swoops down. Then he rises, the fish grasped firmly in his talons, and heads toward a towering Douglas fir.

Once the eagle has vanished into the thick green branches, a wave of delight comes over me. I feel so blessed to have witnessed such a magnificent event. I can't wait to share this experience with my brother. Although, regardless of how enthusiastically I try to repaint the scene, I won't be able to do it justice. Undoubtedly, all Billy will hear is, "Heather saw an eagle."

Whatever work-related tasks Charlie is tending to, I pray he is taking enough time to properly educate Billy on what to expect once we arrive in Cumberland. Billy isn't stupid, and I'm confident he could excel at any job in the right situation. But if his duties don't stimulate his mind, he quickly gives up and veers in the wrong direction.

A chilly wind rushes up the sand and whips around me, stinging my cheeks and hands. Out on the sea, white strokes ride on top of growing swells, a sign that it's time to head back to the cabin.

* * *

The resistance of the wind makes the walk back long and arduous. By the time I reach the steps, my once neatly fastened hair has loosened into a rat's nest. I straighten up as much as possible, then remove my sand-covered boots, and rap on the door.

Soon after, Faye answers. "There's no need for you to knock, Heather. You are family." Inside, she gets a better look at me and starts to laugh. "You look like you got into a fight with the elements and lost."

I laugh with her, knowing I look a mess.

"The men should be back shortly. Let's sit in the living room and talk while we're still alone." Eva plays with wooden blocks on the floor between the two sofas when we sit. Faye looks at me with concern. "Ever since Charlie told me you two were in town and heading for Cumberland, I started worrying. I questioned if maybe you were making a mistake."

I smile. "Oh, don't worry about Billy. He'll catch onto the job, I'm sure. We'll be fine."

"No, Heather. My concern does not lie with your brother. I am more worried about you. Billy is far more adaptable than you are. He's more worldly and knows the ins and outs of life, whereas you have always lived under the umbrella and guidance of your mother. God rest her. After Charlie informed me of your plans, my first thought was that you should stay here while Billy goes to work in the mine. If he manages all right, then once he's set up, you could join him. That way, the risk is on him and not you."

I'm a bit overwhelmed by what she proposes and unsure how to respond. The only thing I'm sure of is I would not feel comfortable staying here. It is not where I belong. Regardless of the mistakes Billy has made, or will probably make again, he's my brother. Sink or swim. We're in this together.

With as much tact as I can muster to avoid offending, I carefully say, "I so appreciate your concern for me, Faye. I really do. But when our mother passed, Billy promised to take care of me until I could manage my own way. And I made a pledge to stick by him. I know your intentions are good, but my place is with my brother right now."

"Did Billy tell you that there's a miner strike right now? That means there could be an uprising in Cumberland, which could get violent."

Billy hadn't mentioned anything about a strike to me. Then again, he wouldn't. He wouldn't want me to get scared. Still, I would have rather found out about it from him and not from our cousin. "I'm sure we'll be safe. My brother would never put me in harm's way."

Faye rolls her eyes and is about to add more to the conversation when Charlie and Billy walk in. I breathe a sigh of relief.

Billy sits beside me and smiles. "Charlie was good enough to enlighten me about working in the mines. I feel much better about everything now."

I force myself not to seem upset with him. "That's great. Did you find out when the train comes through tomorrow?"

"The train usually comes through around eleven," Charlie chimes in. "I can have you both at the platform long before then."

The evening goes relatively smoothly, with Charlie talking about mining and Faye tending to Eva. Everyone goes to bed quite early, giving me no time to speak with Billy about the strike in Cumberland.

Chapter 2

The first rays of dawn break over the calm sea, promising an agreeable day for the journey to our new home. Unable to resist the smell of freshly brewed coffee, Billy dresses quickly and heads to the kitchen. I take my time getting dressed, then make sure the guest room is in order.

Faye meets me in the hallway with a smile. By the look of her neatly pressed skirt and blouse, as well as her perfectly coiffed hair, it's obvious she's been up for hours. If only I had the desire and skills to be as motivated as her, I would get a lot more accomplished in a day. I'm always a step behind and usually running late, a trait I'll need to change if I'll be of use to Billy in Cumberland.

He's the only person worse than me when it comes to tardiness. I'll have to wake him early each day to make sure he's on time. He needs to make a good impression on his new boss.

* * *

On the walk to catch the train, Charlie carries Eva and talks to Billy as Faye and I lag behind.

Faye fixes me with a look. "Remember what I told you, Heather. You're more than welcome to stay here."

"That's very kind of you, Faye. I'll make sure to write to you once we get settled."

As we near the station, thick smoke from the coke ovens permeates the air. Every person passing by waves and smiles at Charlie. He seems to know everyone.

After a short wait, Charlie points to a dark plume of smoke billowing above the tree line. "Train's coming."

We look down the track until the locomotive appears around the bend. As it nears, the hissing of the steam pushing out from the wheels, along with the rhythm of the loud engine, make it almost impossible to hear each other speak. I hug Faye tightly and shake Charlie's hand before climbing aboard the passenger car with Billy toting our bags behind me. Once we're seated on the crowded train, I look out the window and wave goodbye.

I feel the powerful vibrations as the train travels down the track. Thankfully, I have a seat by the window, and even though Billy is squished in next to me, I'm able to turn my head and see the scenery. I catch a final glimpse of the glistening sea before the tracks lead us around a corner and into the forest.

A beautiful palette of greens surrounds us as we motor past a collage of cedar, spruce, and pine trees. The train moves too quickly to focus on anything too long. Soon, the colours of the foliage all meld into one.

Billy leans into me. "Are you okay, sis? You're not nervous, are you?"

I don't make eye contact. "I'm fine."

The truth is, I don't really know how I'm feeling. Since Mother died, I've only felt like half of myself is left. And the half that remains is a mash-up of uncertainty and fear, which has been exaggerated greatly now that I know we may be heading into a dangerous situation.

If only I had some control over my life instead of being completely vulnerable to whatever happens with Billy. My whole future depends on what takes place once we get to Cumberland. The only thread of hope I have is there isn't an uprising when we arrive, and, just maybe, this time, Billy won't screw up and lose another job. If he can be responsible long enough, perhaps I'll be able to find employment and secure my own income.

All I can do now is hope for the best and think positively. Billy has also been impacted by the loss of our mother, and now he is burdened with me. I owe him the benefit of the doubt until he proves me wrong.

Trying not to look obvious, I glance around the passenger car at the other travelers. Most are men as young as me, but there are older ones too. The majority are staring at the ground or looking off into nothingness. It's evident by their worn clothing and lack of enthusiasm on their faces that they are headed to Cumberland for the same reason as my brother, to work in the mines.

* * *

Only after we follow the other passengers off the train can I hear the chatter between them. We follow the herd down a path to a wide street with buildings close together on either side. A wooden sign reading 3rd Street stands at the top of the road.

"I think we need to go to Dunsmuir Avenue." Billy gestures for me to follow. "There's a hotel there. After I get us a room, I can go and find the mining office and speak to the boss."

I ask him about the strike and if we're in any danger.

He turns and forces a grin. "I guess Faye told you about it. Sorry, I never brought it up yesterday because I didn't want you to worry." He stops walking and looks me in the eyes. "I'm not going to let anything happen to you or me, okay? I'm here to work, and if there's any trouble, we'll leave straight away. Worrying about what may or may not happen isn't going to help the situation."

I can tell by the quickness of his speech and quivering voice that he's just as nervous as I am. Still, he's right. There's no point in getting upset now. I guess we'll just take things as they come.

When we reach the top of Dunsmuir Avenue, we stop to get our bearings and look for a hotel sign. Many stores and shops with wooden walkways out front make up the broad avenue. Unlike on 3rd Street, many people are strolling in and out of the buildings.

"There." Billy points to a tall brown building nestled between two others. "There's a sign that says Molly's Hotel."

I follow him halfway down the road until we reach the brown building. There's a wrap-around balcony on the second floor and a large yellow sign hanging above the doorway that reads, *Bed, Bath, and Breakfast.*

We walk up to a long counter, where a tall, thin, elderly man stands. Billy asks if there are any available rooms.

The man looks over his shoulder at a long board with empty metal hooks screwed into it. "Nope. We're all full. You'll have to come back tomorrow or find somewhere else to stay."

My stomach sinks. What if there are no vacant rooms in this town? Where will we stay? My pulse quickens, and my knees start to shake.

Billy looks over at me. "Don't fret. There has to be a room somewhere."

We turn to walk out of the lobby, and just as we reach the door, a woman's voice rings out from behind us. "Hey. Hold on."

Billy and I turn around to see a large woman with wild red hair. She gives us a welcoming grin. "We have a corner room available. The man that checked out this morning forgot to return the key to the front desk."

I breathe a sigh of relief as the woman hands the key to Billy. He shoots me a grin. "See? Everything's going to be fine."

* * *

The room is nothing like the one in the hotel we stayed at in Union Bay. This place has definitely made function over fashion their priority.

After Billy sets down our bags, he walks to the mirror atop the small dresser and finger-combs his hair. "I guess this is as good as it gets today."

"You look fine, brother. Besides, I don't think you're getting hired because of your looks. If that were the case, we'd undoubtedly starve."

Our eyes meet, and we burst into laughter. He shakes his head. "Keep that sense of humour, little sis It may come in handy. I'm going out to find where the mining office is, then speak to the boss and let him know I've arrived."

"How long will you be gone?"

"I'll be back as soon as possible." He hugs me. "It's probably best you wait here for me so I don't have to search the town for you. Besides, you could probably use some time to fix yourself up. You look a little scraggily."

On his way out the door, I grab a pillow off one of the beds and fling it at him. It hits the wall.

"You missed me." He laughs as he closes the door.

Our playfulness lightens my mood and stops my brain from stressing about our situation. I lie back on one of the single beds and close my eyes.

* * *

I wake to the sound of the key in the lock. Just as I'm opening my eyes, Billy comes bounding in.

"We're going to be okay, sis." He's excited. "I met the boss, and he introduced me to the supervisor. They made the job sound pretty straightforward, and apparently, it's been a peaceful protest with the other miners. Not only that, but all the equipment and the tools I need will be taken off my pay, so we don't have to scrape up the money before I start."

"That's great."

"I definitely don't think this will be my dream job, but it'll at least be a way to save money so we can go wherever we want later."

"Did they mention anything about lodgings?"

"Yeah. The boss man said we could move into a cabin in the miner's camp at the edge of town tomorrow. But considering I start work in the morning, you may have to deal with all of that."

"How far away is the mine?"

"It's near a lake about twenty minutes from town. I have to be up before dawn to meet with the crew, then we'll all pile on the back of a wagon that takes us to the mine. Right now, I've got to pick up my gear."

Tired of staying in the room alone, I opt to go along. After I find a warmer sweater in my bag, we head out.

* * *

As soon as we leave the hotel, we see six men pulling a Fire Wheel.

I point to it. "Look at the shape of that rusted old relic. I sure hope there's not a fire."

"I agree. If they had to count on that thing to put out a blaze, these buildings would go down like matchsticks."

We walk south on Dunsmuir Ave and look down the row of shops and businesses. Nothing reminds me of home. No streetcars or new automobiles go by. Still, the place has charm, a welcoming feeling that you don't get in the big city.

As we stroll along, we pass a bakery with the sweet aromas of fresh bread and pastries wafting out the doorway.

Billy inhales deeply. "We'll have to stop in there and get some food on our way back from the supply store."

"There's no rush. I'm too excited to eat right now anyway."

"Hey, maybe you could apply for a job at the bakery." He pauses. "On second thought, that might be a bad idea."

"Why is that?"

"Because you'd eat too many sweets, and before long, you'd be as fat as a mare. Then no one would marry you, and I'd be stuck with you forever."

I giggle. "It's a wonder how you manage to get any attention from the opposite sex."

"I take back what I said, Heather. It wouldn't be all bad if you worked at the bakery and got fat."

"Why is that?"

Billy points across the road to the shop marked *blacksmith*. "You wouldn't have to travel far to get new shoes."

I'm just about to retort with a snappy comeback when Billy stops in front of a shop with bold lettering in the window reading, *Supply Store.* "I think this is where I get my gear. Are you coming inside?"

"I'd rather walk around and look at the shops unless you need help carrying stuff."

"And have you whine all the way back to the hotel? No thanks."

I smile. "You're a real hoot today."

Billy kisses me on the forehead, then tells me not to wander too far.

The next storefront has pretty pink flowers painted on the windows. I look up and see *Dressmaker* etched into a sign on the door. When I walk in, I notice a woman of about thirty arranging displays of dresses and accessories.

She gives me a kind smile. "May I help you look for something?"

"I'm just browsing, thank you."

The woman returns to her work as I peruse the racks. The garments here are much the same in the way of dark colours as I saw ladies wearing in Union Bay. If the women wore lighter colours here, as they do in Vancouver, all their time would be spent doing laundry.

I thank the woman for letting me mull about, then exit the shop. Back on the walkway, I look up the street but can't see Billy, so I keep exploring.

I walk past a furniture store and a tobacco shop and then decide to cross the road. I am heading down the ramp when I see two young policemen leaning against a building. They're talking and smoking cigarettes. My eyes meet theirs as I walk by.

Then their attention shifts to a man walking down the center of the street. He's thin with scraggly hair, and based on his unkempt dirty jacket and pants, I assume he's homeless. The police intently watch the man as he walks down Dunsmuir Avenue and disappears between two buildings. Moments later, the police officers extinguish their cigarettes and walk briskly in the direction of the man.

It's common to see police officers on the streets of Vancouver. Usually, they're walking around in the busy areas of downtown. But here in Cumberland, a working town, the long coats and shiny gold buttons of a police uniform stick out like a sore thumb.

When I reach the other side of the street, I hear Billy call my name. I turn to see him heading toward me with a large canvas bag slung over one shoulder.

He hands me money, then suggests I buy us some food and meet him back in the hotel room.

I stare into the long display case, my eyes scanning the tall cupcakes with pastel pink icing, soft puffy pastries with colorful sprinkles, and flaky plump sausage rolls. I order two of each, then ask the baker for a French roll from a basket on the counter.

The large, elderly woman looks at me intently as she boxes up the sizable order. "I've never seen you here before."

"I'm from Vancouver. My brother and I just arrived earlier today."

She looks suddenly smug. "Let me guess. Your brother has come to work in the mines."

"Yes. That's right."

The woman shakes her head. "I guess if scabs keep coming, there will never be an end to the strike."

"Scabs?"

"Yeah, scabs. People who cross protest lines and take the jobs of hard-working men fighting to get a better wage."

I can't help but feel offended. "Ma'am. When my brother secured the job, he wasn't informed about the strike. In fact, he didn't learn about it until we were in Union Bay."

"Maybe so, but once he did, he should've hightailed it back to where he came from."

"That really wasn't an option for us."

She finishes with my order and takes my money. After she makes change, she passes it to me and looks into my eyes. "Look, you're young. I'm sure your brother is, too. I didn't mean to treat you harshly. But a lot of families are suffering because the miners dared to take a stand against the mining company."

"I'm sorry about the workers and their families, and I'm sure my brother is as well. We know nothing about the politics of what's happening here."

"I'm sure you don't. Just tell your brother to keep his eyes open and watch out for himself. He won't be making much pay, and with the hours he'll put in, you'll barely see him. Not to mention, he'll have to endure all the name-calling and verbal abuse by the miners on the picket lines. They're good men, but they don't like the sight of new workers coming in to steal their jobs."

I take my order from the counter. "I understand."

I'm just about at the door when the woman stops me. "What's your brother's name?"

"It's Billy."

"What does he look like?"

What a strange question. Why does she want to know what my brother looks like? I'm too surprised to think of a way out of the question, so I describe him.

The baker nods. "My son is protesting up at the mine. I'll give him the description of your brother, see they can go a bit easy on him, considering he wasn't told of the strike before he was hired."

I thank the woman and quickly leave the shop.

When I reach the hotel, I stop in the lobby for a few minutes before continuing upstairs. I need to process the unexpected confrontation I just had at the bakery.

In the room, Billy is lying on one of the beds, reading the paper. "Hey, sis. What took you so long? I'm starving."

I place the baked goods on the bed. "I went to the bakery and got trapped in the weirdest conversation with the woman there."

Billy sets down the newspaper and sits up. "Why was it weird?"

I tell him what the baker said and how miserable she was to me initially. Then I explain that her son is on the picket line. "She said she would speak to him and have him go easy on you."

Billy laughs and shakes his head. "If you believe that, you're just as crazy as the baker."

"Why is that?"

"Picket lines with disgruntled workers don't give a damn about the individuals taking their jobs, I can assure you."

I shrug. "You may be right. I just hope there isn't any violence."

"Those men are literally fighting for their lives, Heather. I'm sure most of them go to bed with hungry bellies. If they have wives and children, that makes it all the worse."

I sit down on the bed. A wave of guilt comes over me as I look at the box of food.

Billy puts his hand on my shoulder. "You can't worry about it. They are on their journey, and we are on ours. Things will work out the way they are meant to."

"I guess you're right."

It takes me a while, but eventually, I can eat. When the box is empty, and all that remains are traces of powdered sugar on our hands and mouths, Billy washes up and tells me he needs to go to sleep, as he'll be getting up before dawn.

"I've written down the address to the housing office you must go to in the morning. Someone there will take you to the miner's camp and show you which cabin is ours."

* * *

I wake to the sound of continuous tapping on the window. I stretch, then get up and walk over to look outside. Angry clouds churn overhead as rain runs down the window.

Billy's bed is made, and the canvas bag full of supplies is gone. I wish I had awakened before he left. I wanted to give him some positive words before he started work.

I sigh. I hope his day isn't unbearable and the striking miners don't intimidate him.

I dress in accordance with the miserable weather, opting for my warmest clothes. After putting up my hair, I grab the address to the housing office and head out.

From looking out the window upstairs, I didn't predict just how angry the weather was outside. Wind whips down the wide street, carrying sheets of hard rain. The dirt roads are littered with muddy puddles, making the task of walking challenging and unpleasant. With my head down and eyes focused on maneuvering through the thick muck, I make my way to 3rd Street. Once there, I can use the elevated walkways, making it easier to read the shop signs and navigate to the miner's housing company.

* * *

The office is small, with one long counter and stacks of paper on every available surface. At first, I don't see anyone. Then I spot a feeble old man sitting at a small desk in the corner, his face buried in a large folder.

"Excuse me, sir. I'm here to arrange lodgings."

The man looks over the top of the folder. "We only house miners, and you sure don't look like one of them."

I smile. "No, sir. My brother Billy is a miner. He gave me your address and assured me that you could help find us a cabin in the camp."

The man sighs as though this is a great inconvenience, then slowly stands and walks over to a tall stack of papers. After he grabs a page from the top, he grumbles, "Do you have a pencil?"

I shake my head. The man sighs even louder and looks around the piles. Finally, he locates a pencil and walks over to me. "Here. Fill out this form and hand it back to me. Once that's done, I'll take you to the cabins."

Very carefully, I slide over a pile of papers on the counter. Then, with just enough room for the form, I do my best to fill in the blanks.

With about as much enthusiasm as a sloth, the old codger takes my paper, then inaudibly mumbles as he reads it aloud. I'm glad Billy isn't here with me because all it would take is one glance at each other, and we wouldn't be able to control our laughter.

After the man reads the form, he nods curtly. "I'll take you to the cabins and show you which one is yours."

I wait for what seems like forever as he shuffles around the office and gathers his jacket, hat, and walking stick. He motions for me to step outside, then follows me through the door. When the strong wind hits, the man wobbles dangerously before steadying himself with the cane.

I follow as he ambles along the walkway, then takes a sharp left between two buildings. When we come out the other side, he heads for a buggy with a mare hooked up to it. The horse looks just as thin and feeble as the old man.

Once we're seated in the buggy, he whistles, and the horse slowly moves. On account of the rain, coupled with the fact that we're travelling around the town center, I don't get to see much of the downtown core.

Finally, we pull up to a large group of small houses. My grumbling chauffeur and I climb out of the buggy. Although I could've gotten here faster walking backwards with my ankles tied, I appreciate the efforts of the elderly man and his old nag.

"This is the miner's camp." The old guy points to a modest little cabin on our left. "Your place is just over there."

Three wooden steps lead to the front door with a window on either side. The man passes me the key and says to have a look around. It's obvious he wouldn't fare well climbing the stairs.

As soon as I open the door, I see how small the cabin is. The front room is understated: four walls, a fireplace, a wood stove, and a small table with two chairs in the corner.

At the back of the main room are two doors. I cross the room and open the first door. Inside is a single wood-framed bed resting under a small window. The next room is much the same—plain but clean and habitable.

On my way out of the cabin, I mentally note the missing essentials I'll need to get—coverings for the windows, a rug for the entranceway, pots, pans, and dishware. Not to mention towels, bedding, and cleaning essentials. That being said, I'm pleasantly surprised at how clean the cabin is and look forward to the challenge of making this a cozy little home for Billy and me.

Once outside, I notice the rain has picked up, and the old man and horse are sopping wet. I apologize for inconveniencing the man and for making him endure the downpour. He says nothing in return, only grumbles.

When I'm seated back in the buggy, I look up. White signs with black writing and arrows painted on them are attached to a pole. With the rain blurring my vision, the only sign I can make out clearly says *China Town*.

Thankfully, the old horse is keener on going home than on the journey here. We make it back to the housing office in half the time it took to get to the cabins. I thank the old man one last time, give the horse a few pats on the neck, then head back to Dunsmuir Avenue to price out items we will need for the cabin.

* * *

Desperate to escape the rain, I duck into the first shop. Drops of water puddle on the floor beneath me as I look around, and then see an older, dark-haired man leaning over a long bench, a small tool in one hand and a boot in the other.

He looks up and smiles, his crystal blue eyes welcoming and kind. "Can I help you with something, young lady? Or did you just come in to wash the floor?"

I look down at the rapidly growing puddle at my feet. "I'm so sorry. It's miserable out there."

The man smiles forgivingly, immediately reminding me of a grandpa character in the storybooks Mother read to me as a child. "I take it you're from someplace else?"

I nod, then tell him how my brother and I just arrived from Vancouver and why we came.

Unlike the bakery lady, he doesn't react when I mention that Billy came here to work in the mine amidst the strike. "What's your name?"

"Oh, forgive me, my name is Heather."

He reaches toward me and, with a hand the size of a plate, shakes mine. "I'm Lou. Did the company get you set up with lodgings yet?"

"Yes. I've just been to see the cabin. It was small, but my brother and I were used to living in a close-knit space. I was going to find some essentials for the cabin when I walked into your shop."

Lou is generous with his knowledge about which store has the best prices for bedding and dishes.

"Thank you for your kindness." I gesture to the puddle on the floor. "I will leave and let you get back to your work, but first, I'd like to clean up the mess I've made."

"Don't worry about that. It'll dry on its own."

As I exit the shop, I look up and read the cobbler's sign—*Lyster's Shoe Repair*. Even though I feel bad for interrupting him, I feel grateful to have met such a kind soul. In the future, I will make a point of waving to Lou when I pass by his shop.

Once back on the walkway, finding the housewares shop Lou suggested doesn't take long, and I can duck out of the rain again.

The odour of lavender breezes past me as I enter, reminding me of the quaint little boutiques around Vancouver. I note what things cost as I look at dishes, cutlery, and cookware. In the back of the shop are shelves with patchwork quilts, wool blankets, and pillows. Pricing out the most basic linens, I do my best to tally up the bill.

It's a lot more than I had thought. I will have to bring the cost of our needs up to Billy gently. I don't want to overwhelm him when he just started working.

* * *

The rain fades and takes with it the powerful wind. Encouraging beams of sunshine burst through the dark clouds, illuminating the water-drenched street.

I notice a café sign on the opposite side of the street and suddenly crave a hot cup of tea and a biscuit. After navigating across the muddy road, I reach the café and do my best to kick the mud off my boots before entering.

Inside, there are oodles of people sit on stools at the counter or chairs at small tables. I walk down the aisle to an empty stool at the end of the counter. Thankfully, pegs are on the wall nearby to hang my wet coat. After I sit down, a friendly waitress approaches and takes my order.

A man wearing a blue pressed suit and a stylish tie sits on the stool next to me. *He's obviously a local businessman*, I think to myself.

When the waitress brings my tea and biscuit, she hands the man a newspaper. As I sip my hot drink, I watch the man open the paper. I immediately see the large, bold-print headline—*The Threat of Violence at Mine #4.*

My heart sinks, and my cup rattles in its saucer. Filled with concern for Billy, I'm in no mood to finish my tea. I decide to order a sandwich to go, as I'm sure Billy will be hungry when he gets off work in a couple of hours.

While waiting for my order, the man beside me walks out, leaving his paper behind. I grab it and thumb past the mining story to the next page, an article about burglaries occurring up and down the coastline. There isn't any information about the criminals who travel by boat under the cover of darkness. Some victims claimed to have heard a loud engine on the water shortly after the burglaries.

As I read on, I learned the police chief out of Nanaimo had declared war on the criminals after locals demanded something be done. Many stores and businesses between Nanaimo and Comox were hit, sometimes more than once. The Union Bay Store had suffered losses twice already.

"Are you reading about the boat bandits?"

I glance up to see the waitress standing with a wrapped sandwich in her hand. I nod. "Yes. It's quite shocking."

"A few of my regulars who do business up and down the coast said the robberies have everyone on high alert. From what I've heard, some residents living near the water are ready to take matters into their own hands."

I shake my head. "I don't blame them. They have a right to protect their families and their valuables."

The waitress nods and hands me the bill.

I set the money down for the food. "Do you mind if I take the newspaper with me? I'm hoping there are job listings posted in the paper."

"Go ahead."

* * *

A group of children hollers and laughs in the street as they take turns jumping in the mucky puddles. Their joy is contagious, and I can't help but smile, even though I'm sure they will be reprimanded once their mothers see their soiled clothing.

Back in the room, I put the sandwich on the dresser, then change out of my damp clothing and sit on the bed with the newspaper. I carefully scan the job listings, but other than a few farmhand positions, all I find is a help-wanted ad from a courier service in town. I carefully tear it out and slide the paper into my pocket. After Billy goes to work tomorrow, I'll make myself presentable, then go and see about the job.

I hear the slow footsteps on the wood floor echoing up the hall. The door opens, and standing in front of me is a person covered in coal dust.

I wouldn't recognize my brother if it weren't for his brilliant blue eyes. He looks well past his years with the black dust embedded in every little line on his face. His hair, eyebrows, and little chin stubble are filled with the stuff.

"Oh, Billy. You should see yourself. You're filthy."

"You didn't think I was going to come home all gussied up, did you?" His voice is slow and raspy.

"How did it go?"

"From the moment I arrived at the mine, it was hell. The strikers were calling us names and throwing things at us. Our only escape was to travel deep into the cold, dark mine. It was hell."

"That's terrible. I'm so sorry."

He drops his canvas bag to the floor. "I just want to lie on the bed and sleep."

"Please, Billy. You need to go and have a wash, and then you can eat the sandwich I bought you. You'll get run down if you don't take care of yourself. Besides, all that coal dust you're wearing can't be good for you."

He sighs and, without saying a word, turns and ambles out of the room.

I quickly turn down the covers on his bed, then open the parcel with his sandwich and arrange a napkin and a glass of water beside it.

Billy's face is still stained in spots from the dust when he returns, though the wash has perked him up enough to eat. Famished, he devours the thick sandwich in a few huge bites.

I leave the room while he gets ready for bed. When I come back in, he's already lying down. I tell him about the cabin and the essentials we need to buy, but I can see he's only absorbing part of what I'm saying. Soon after, he's snoring.

I lie quietly on my cot and stare out the window into the dark night. I'm so proud of my brother. Granted, he's only worked one shift so far, but his exhaustion shows how he'd put everything into the job. If my parents could see him right now, they would be thrilled with how hard Billy is being responsible. Our mother, especially, would take pride in knowing that her efforts in raising us eventually paid off.

Our father was not the best role model for Billy. Dad was a jack-of-all-trades and found sporadic jobs around Vancouver that barely paid the rent. Not the best example of how a man and father should be. I scarcely remember him, though I do recall the arguments after he'd arrive home late with empty pockets and the pungent stench of whiskey on his breath.

I was only seven when two policemen came to the door and asked to speak to my mother in private. A few moments later, I heard her sobbing from the front door. Later that evening, Billy told me our father was on the wrong end of a drunken argument.

It was a few years before I learned the details of that night. How he had been stabbed in the neck with a broken bottle and died in an alleyway outside a downtown bar. Occasionally, after seeing my mother exhausted from working a fourteen-hour day, I would resent my father for leaving her with the burden of raising us alone.

But, in a true testament to my mother's positive disposition, she never spoke an ill word about him. Instead, she would say, "There is nothing we can do about what has already happened. All we can do now is focus on the future."

Chapter 3

Coming out of a deep sleep, I keep my eyes closed and listen for the sound of another rainy day, but all is still and quiet outside the window.

I open my eyes and look over at the cot next to me. Billy is gone, probably toiling in the pit of the mine already.

He looked so miserable when he came home yesterday. I wanted to cheer him up, but it was no use. He was too exhausted. Also, since he'd likely not heard me talk about the cabin necessities, my hands were tied getting us set up at the new place. We don't even have bedding.

However, upon standing, I notice a note on the dresser and an envelope beside it. Billy's writing is sloppy, undoubtedly due to exhaustion from the day before.

Don't worry about me, little sis. I'm sure my shift will go better today. I've left some money for you in the envelope. Use it for what we need to get set up. I will see you after work. Love Billy.

I smile as I pick up the envelope and thumb through the thin stack of bills. There isn't enough here to get everything we'll need to move into the cabin, so I'll have to stick to the basics for now.

I quickly dress and head to the shops, excited to be one step closer to moving out of the hotel.

* * *

The glow of the sun casts a sepia hue over everything. Crossing the street with only pocket-sized puddles remaining from yesterday's storm is much easier.

I look in the window when I come to the cobbler's place. Lou is working away inside, and I give him a quick wave and a smile.

Now that the weather is better, more people are on the walkway, specifically more women, with most men at work for the day.

At the housewares shop, I select some of the same items I picked out yesterday, then tell the storekeeper which cabin to deliver to tomorrow. With the task of shopping taking up less time than expected, I pull the ad I'd torn out of the paper yesterday from my pocket. Determined, I head off to find the courier to see about a job.

* * *

Unlike the other shops in town, there are no windows on this one, only a small sign on the door with two names, *Shirley's Weaving* and *Cumberland Courier.*

As soon as I step inside, I notice a large wooden structure with lots of fabric and string hooked up to it. A sign on the wall has an arrow pointing to a closed door. I walk to the door, knock twice, and wait.

After a few long moments, the door opens. Before me is a thick woman with wide shoulders, wearing a men's style shirt and baggy trousers. She looks me up and down. "What can I do for you?" Her voice sounds husky.

I try to answer her, but my words are stuck. I've never seen a lady wearing men's clothing in public before.

"Well?"

Finally, my tongue unties. "My name is Heather. I've come to see about the courier job listed in the paper."

"Do you have any experience with the job? How about operating a horse and buggy?"

I shake my head. "No on both accounts, but I'm a fast learner and a hard worker."

She hums and haws for a moment. "You're not very big. Some of the items I transport can get pretty heavy."

"I think it would surprise you at the amount of weight I can pack. Some of my jobs in the city required me to carry very heavy boxes."

"Well, the job doesn't officially start for another couple of weeks. If you come back then, I guess I could give you a try."

I exhale with relief. "That's perfect. You'll see me back here in two weeks, and I'll be raring to go."

"I hope so." She stretches. "Now that we have that sorted out, I've got to get back to work."

"Okay. I won't take up any more of your time. See you in two weeks."

Just as the woman is about to close the door, I ask her name.

"It's Betty."

"Nice to meet you, Betty."

The door closes, and I walk toward the entrance. Just as I reach out to grab the knob, the door opens, and a blond lady with crystal blue eyes steps inside. She smiles at me. "Can I help you with something?"

I explain how I came to speak with the courier, Betty.

"Ah, yes, she is looking for a new employee. The last worker had to leave after the strikes started. She and her husband couldn't sustain a living on her salary alone. A common story around these parts lately."

"That's awful. I hope her husband found work someplace else."

"Yes. I believe he had an offer at another mine up north. Anyway, she's gone now, and you're here."

I smile. "My name is Heather. What's yours?"

"Shirley."

"Are you an employee here?"

"No. I own the business. I make rugs on that machine and sell them in town or ship them elsewhere."

"Wow. That's really neat. That machine looks pretty complicated with all the levers and wires."

"It's pretty easy once you know what you're doing."

Shirley is an amiable and personable lady. It suddenly occurs to me that she might ask about my story and how I came to be in Cumberland. As much as I enjoy talking with her, I know if I mention that my brother is a scab up at the mine, her kindly demeanor toward me could change.

I tell her it is nice to meet her, but I should be going. "I've got a few more errands to run."

"Of course. Congratulations on your new job. I'm sure we'll see more of each other."

I breathe a huge sigh of relief as I exit the shop. Not only have I bought the cabin's bare essentials, but I have secured a job— all in one day! I can't wait to tell Billy.

I walk the same route back to the hotel. As I pass the cobbler's, I see a young man about my age sweeping the front entrance. When I get closer, old Lou comes out with a smile. "Hello, Heather. It's nice to see you again. This here is my grandson, Stewart. He's helping me out at the shop today."

For the first time, I look directly at the young man. His hair is bright red and disheveled, and the only thing more pronounced than his skinny, crooked nose is the pair of enormous ears. Stewart briefly looks at me, and when our eyes meet, his pale face turns a bright tomato red.

I smile at him. "Nice to meet you."

He gives no response.

Lou nudges the young man. "After we met yesterday, I thought maybe my grandson here could show you around Cumberland. He knows the place well. He was born and raised here."

"That's very kind of you to offer, but I'll be quite busy getting my brother and myself set up at the cabin. Maybe some other time."

"Okay, then. It's a date. Just as soon as you find some free time, come on back, and the two of you can—"

"Great. That sounds fine." I edge around them. "See you later."

Once I cross the street, I shake my head. That was so awkward and uncomfortable, not only for me but for the poor grandson. He was so shy. I thought he was going to pass out.

As I stroll along Dunsmuir Ave, I pop into a few different stores. I load up on penny candy at a sweet shop, then browse for twenty minutes in a general store. Then, with hours before Billy gets home, I go inside a sporting goods store that carries everything from guns to fishing rods. Not my first choice to browse, but it helps pass the time.

Once my feet start to get tired, I decide to head back to the hotel. On the way, I keep my eyes open for a restaurant. Remembering how famished Billy was after work yesterday, I pop into the first place I see—a place called *Chinese Noodle House*—and order a combination dish and ask them to wrap it up.

While carrying the food through the hotel lobby, I notice posters on a board by the front desk. The first poster is advertising an upcoming play called *The Grand Duchess* at the local theatre this weekend.

I'll have to ask Billy if we can afford to go. Seeing a live show could be just what he needs to take his mind off the dismal reality of his new job, and it would be a pleasant diversion for me.

I love to watch plays and have since a child. Even though we were living paycheck to paycheck, at least once a year, my mother would dress me up with pretty bows in my hair and a dress she'd made from one of her old outfits, and we would take the streetcar to the theater downtown. We always had a wonderful time.

The second poster advertises a Fall Dance held in The Cumberland Hall at month's end. I love that there are local events to bring the community together. At least this town isn't sleepy and idle.

Upstairs, I sit on the bed and write out a to-do list for tomorrow. I'm sure I'll be busy arranging the cabin after the store delivers the things I've ordered. When I'm done writing, I open my bags and refold everything so I'm ready to check out of the room in the morning.

Billy walks in an hour later. Although he's not half as exhausted looking as he was yesterday, he's just as filthy.

"How was your day?"

"I lived through it."

He sets his work bag on the floor and heads out to get cleaned up. In the meantime, I arrange our dinner, which is now room temperature. I put one box on Billy's bed and one on mine.

After a few minutes, Billy returns. His face is clean enough to identify him, but the coal dust is still embedded in his ears, the fine lines of his neck, and around his eyes.

I give him a few minutes to relax and start eating his dinner. Then I tell him about my day and how I bought as much for the cabin as possible with the money he gave me. Then I tell him about finding the ad in the paper for a courier job and how I went and checked it out today.

"Wow, you were busy." He shovels another bite in. "But don't get your hopes up about the job. Many people in this town are looking for employment, and they're probably a lot more physically capable of handling the weight of parcels and boxes than you are."

"That's what my new boss initially thought, as well."

He shifts his focus from his food to me. "New boss?"

"I got the job. The owner, Betty, told me to see her in two weeks, and she'll hire me."

Billy shakes his head. "I must admit I'm quite shocked that you were hired on the spot. But I think it's great, even if you end up getting fired after the first day."

"That's a terrible thing to say. Why would I get fired?"

"Because you're a wimp. I'd bet anything you won't be able to do the job physically."

I push my food away. "I'm beginning to get steamed up."

He scoffs. "Heather, to date, your jobs haven't been labor-intensive ones. You're great at cleaning and—"

"That's enough. I'll just have to show you what I'm made of."

"Okay. Take the job. It's your back, not mine." He grins.

It takes me a few minutes to calm down. I try to remember he's probably being an ass because he's tired from working so many hours. Knowing he'll likely go straight to bed after he eats, I ask him to tell me about the mine and how things work.

"I don't feel much like talking about working in that dark pit."

"Okay, tell me about the other miners."

"I've only talked to a few of them on break. What do you want to know?"

"I don't know. Are the men you work with all from Canada or other places?"

"We never really got into it, but I heard a couple of guys speaking with a British accent. There are also a few Chinese men on my crew, the poor buggers."

"Why do you say that?"

"Because they're treated very unfairly compared to us whites."

"In what way?"

"Lack of proper pay, for one. The Chinese men only make a third of what us whites do, and they do the exact same job."

"That can't be right. Are you sure someone's not pulling your leg?"

"I wish it wasn't true, Heather. But it is."

"But I'm sure they have families to feed, too. How can the mining company get away with that?"

Billy finishes his dinner and climbs into bed. "I'm not a politician, or a lawyer. I have no idea how the company can legally or morally do what they do. All I am is a scab, a grunt worker. My job is to bust my back in that mine, not solve social issues."

When the room is dark, and I can hear Billy's slow breathing, I lay my head on the pillow, my eyes wide open and a sick feeling in the pit of my stomach over what I just heard. Even though I'm in no way connected to the company, I feel a sense of guilt.

* * *

For once, I wake in time to say goodbye to Billy before he leaves for work. He hands me a few more bills and tells me to pick up some groceries. "Do what you can to set up the cabin today. I'll get let off there after work."

Outside the window, the dark sky holds onto what's left of the night. I reread the out-of-date newspaper and wait for daylight to break. Filled with the anticipation of moving into the cabin, I soon become restless and pace the room.

When the first spark of dawn shines through the window, I pile Billy's bags in the corner with mine, then head down to the lobby to inquire about transportation.

Thankfully, the grumpy old codger isn't working. Instead, a kindly man about forty is wiping down the counter and getting ready to start the day. I walk up and tell him that my brother and I will be checking out today, then ask if there is any form of transportation I could take to the miners' cabins. He shakes his head just as the lobby doors open, and a young gentleman walks in.

The two men give a quick nod of familiarity, then start talking. I wait patiently as the front desk man seems to forget about me. Finally, I clear my throat loudly, and both men stop talking and look at me.

"I don't mean to interrupt, but I was asking if you knew where I might be able to get a ride with my luggage to the miners' cabins."

"Yes. That's right. No, I'm sorry, ma'am. I don't know of—"

"I've got nothing to do yet," the second man interrupts. "I can take you there if you like."

I sigh in relief, thank the man, and hurry upstairs to get the bags.

It takes two trips to carry both mine and Billy's things downstairs. Once I hand in the room key, the other man grabs Billy's bags, and I take mine.

The horse and carriage are much nicer than the one I rode in yesterday. And instead of having that grouchy old codger driving me, this man is happy-go-lucky and, like me, enjoys talking. By the time we reach the cabin, I've learned all about when he first moved here, how many children he has, and which café is his wife's favorite. After he helps me inside with the luggage, I thank him for his generosity and say goodbye.

Once the door is closed, I notice the chilliness in the room. I quickly look in the bottom of the cabinet fixed into the wall, hoping I'll find a few pieces of coal left over from the last tenants, but there's only black dust. Billy won't be home for hours, and it's too long of a walk to get new coal. Besides, I don't want to risk missing the delivery. The only way I will stay warm is if I keep moving.

I'm just about to pick up the luggage by the door when I glimpse someone walking this way through the window, carrying a small canvas bag. I'd recognize that messy red hair anywhere. It's Stewart, the cobbler's grandson.

What is he doing down here? It's quite a jaunt from his grandfather's shop. I move out of view, then peek out of the window, only to see him walking up the steps.

I duck out of sight, hoping he didn't see me. If he knocks, I'll pretend no one is home. I'm far too busy unpacking and getting settled to waste time socializing. Not to mention, it's highly inappropriate for him to be stopping by my home when I don't even know him.

When I met Stewart yesterday, he was painfully shy. He raps on the door. I push my back against the wall and stay perfectly still. I'm sure if I don't answer, he'll skedaddle.

I wait and listen but hear nothing. Five minutes go by, then ten, and still no further sound from outside. Feeling like I'm finally in the clear, I rise and peek out the small window on the door. A scream escapes my lips when I see Stewart's face looking back at me.

I'm frozen for a few moments, shaking, my heart thumping like it's going to jump out of my chest. Then, my fear turns to anger. I turn the knob and pull open the door. "Stewart. You scared the living daylights out of me. What are you doing here?"

Almost immediately, I regret my outburst. Stewart's hands are shaking. My anger has rattled him so badly that he struggles to speak.

I keep my tone soft and sigh. "Look, I'm sorry. You just really scared me. What is it you've come for?"

He stares at his feet. "My grandfather told me to come down here and make sure you didn't need any help setting things up."

I smile. "Well, that was very kind of Lou and you, but I've got things under control."

He holds up the small bag. "Here's some coal, in case you didn't have a chance to get any yet. It's best to light the stove and not the fireplace—it will heat up the cabin better."

"Thank you. It is quite cold in here."

By the look on Stewart's face, I can see his disappointment that he couldn't be more useful, especially after he trekked all the way here.

"You know what, Stewart? You seem to know a lot more about where to light the coal. Maybe I could use some help."

His gaze lifts from the ground, and he straightens up.

I show him to the stove. At first, I hover over him as he opens the stove and unties the bag of coal. However, when I notice his hands trembling, I assume my presence makes him nervous, so I return my attention to putting mine and Billy's luggage away in the bedrooms.

When I return to the front room, Stewart stands at the entrance with the door wide open. I walk up behind him. "Are you leaving now?"

He shakes his head and points outside. "I think your delivery is arriving."

Sure enough, there's a buggy out front with items in the back. Stewart and I meet the delivery man on the steps, and the three of us take armloads into the cabin until the buggy is empty.

Stewart walks out with the delivery man and chats while I stand, looking at the pile on the floor. It will take time to get things sorted, and I still need to head downtown to buy groceries before Billy gets home. Thankfully, it's still early.

Just as I bend down and grab an armful of linens, Stewart walks in. "Heather, I was just thinking. You may need a dresser or two for the bedrooms and a cabinet for this room." His voice is quiet, still shy.

"Yes. You're right. And as the money comes in, I can add more things."

Stewart clears his throat. "I can get you those things for free if you'd like."

"How so?"

"When miners move out of the cabins, sometimes they leave stuff behind. Then, if the new tenant doesn't want them, the things are stored in a building in town."

"That would really help us, but I wouldn't want to put you in any trouble."

"No trouble. I know the delivery guy. I asked him, and he said he would help get the furniture and bring it here."

I smile. "I don't know what to say. That's very kind of both of you."

I'm overwhelmed by the generosity of both young men. However, if Billy knows we've gotten donated furniture, he may be upset. Mother used to say he is too proud for his own good. Nevertheless, if no one is using the furniture, I can't think of any good reason why we shouldn't be using it.

* * *

The cabin is cozy and warm, thanks to Stewart's efforts. I've done all I can until the men return with the furniture. Once they do, I'll have places to put the rest of the things away.

Outside comes the sound of a child laughing, and I walk over to the side window to investigate. A girl, maybe about four, runs around in circles between the cabins as a shaggy puppy chases her. I laugh when the pup tugs at the child's coat, making the little girl screech and giggle. Thankfully, the puppy isn't aggressive and seems to understand the game. Around and around they go until the child loses her balance and falls. She lands hard on the ground and lets out an ear-piercing scream.

I wait for a parent or someone to appear, but no one comes to her rescue. I hurry out the front door and around the side of the cabin to help the child.

I'm a few feet away when a woman opens the door of the nearest cabin and runs toward us. I reach down to help the child just as the woman arrives and lifts the girl to her feet.

The pup ambles up behind them, and the woman kicks it. "Shoo. Get lost, you stupid dog!"

The woman's anger fades as she turns to me. "Thank you for coming to help. If I had a gun in the cabin, I'd shoot that mongrel mutt."

"I was watching your little girl as she ran around. The pup seemed to be playing gently with her."

"Doesn't matter if it was. That dirty thing has been hanging around for days, whining and crying for food. I've got three little mouths to feed, plus my husband and me. The last bloody thing I need is that fleabag begging for food all the time."

Immediately, I don't like the woman. My brother and I were raised to be kind and compassionate to wayward dogs and cats. My mother would save whatever scraps we had left over from dinner, and she and I would carry them down to the alleyway to feed the homeless animals.

The woman glares at the pup. "Maybe I will speak to my husband when he gets home and see if he can borrow a shotgun to handle the problem."

I want to tell her exactly what I think of her cruelty, but I don't want to create tension when I've barely moved in yet. "Actually, there's no need to shoot the dog. I can care for the pup until I find him a home." I force a smile on my face.

She scoffs. "Do whatever you like. Just keep it away from me and my kids." She carries her child inside.

I bend down and slowly extend my hand to the puppy. At first, he's cautious, but after a few moments, he sniffs my hand, then inches closer. Within minutes, I'm petting the creature, and he's jumping up on me.

"Don't worry, little guy. I won't let that mean old hag hurt you."

Thankfully, the dog follows when I stand up and head for the cabin, so I don't have to figure out a leash. As I walk, the toe of my boot kicks a small rock, sending it rolling. Instantly, the pup jumps forward and finds the rock, then picks it up in his mouth and carries it back to me.

"That's a clever trick." I pat him on the head.

The sound of wheels comes down the road, and I look up to see the delivery wagon coming this way. I walk into the cabin and prop the front door open, then make sure there aren't any tripping obstacles for the men. My new fluffy friend follows close behind me.

Stewart walks into the cabin backwards. He has one end of a tall, five-drawer dresser, and the delivery man has the other end. As they maneuver the piece of furniture through the main room and into my room, Stewart just about trips over the puppy. His confused eyes meet mine.

I sigh. "It's a long story. I'll tell you later."

Next off the wagon is a shorter dresser with three long drawers for Billy's room. The last item is a two-door cabinet with a top drawer for cutlery and utensils.

After they set the cabinet up against the wall, they take a moment to catch their breath.

I lay a hand against the cabinet. "I can't believe the work you two did. The furniture couldn't be more perfect. Thank you so much. I wish I had something for you to drink, but I must go shopping."

The delivery guy wipes his forehead. "The furniture is a bit dirty. You'll have to wipe everything down, and a couple of drawers in one of the dressers will require readjusting."

"That's no problem at all. We're better off now that we have something to put our clothes into."

Stewart gestures to his friend. "He has to do more deliveries now. But we can get dropped off downtown if you need to pick up some groceries."

As much as I want to wipe down the furniture and put away the rest of the things, instead, I take them up on their offer because it's such a long way to walk.

Stewart, the pup, and I all climb into the back of the delivery wagon. As we ride toward Dunsmuir Avenue, I tell Stewart about the gun-happy neighbor and the pup.

"Does your brother like dogs?"

"Yes, and if he weren't highly allergic to them, he would've had one while we were growing up."

"Will he be cross with you when he sees the dog?"

"Probably." I shrug. "But I'll explain that the puppy will only stay until I can find a suitable home. My brother will understand. I'll have to keep the dog in my room and out of Billy's way."

When we reach downtown, Stewart helps me off the wagon and the pup jumps down behind me.

"I'd like to tag along and help you carry your groceries home if that's okay," Stewart says.

I laugh. "Aren't you sick of me yet?"

He shakes his head, a slight grin on his face. "I just have to check in with my grandpa and make sure he doesn't need me to do anything first."

As we walk toward Lou's shop, I glance at Stewart. "When you showed up at the cabin this morning, you would barely look at me. I couldn't get you to say more than a few words at a time. Now, you're communicating with ease. Why is that?"

He shrugs, a flush creeping up his neck. "I don't know. I've always been shy around people I don't know."

"Well, I'm glad you're feeling more at ease with me now."

With the dog in tow, we arrive at the cobbler. Lou is standing over the long bench, working on a pair of men's boots. Stewart and I both say hello, but all of Lou's focus is on the puppy.

"And where did you come from, little fella?" Lou leans down to pet the dog.

"Heather found him around the cabins. We're pretty sure he's a stray."

"He probably is, and God knows how long it's been since he's had a meal." Lou reaches his hand into a tall glass jar with biscuits in it. The pup crunches down on the biscuit, and just like that, it's gone.

"I was thinking of going with Heather to get some groceries, then helping her home. Unless you have anything that needs doing."

Lou smiles at both me and his grandson. "Nope. You two carry on. I've got everything under control here."

We say goodbye and open the door to walk out. I turn back and look at the pup, who isn't following us. "Come on, puppy. Leave Lou to work."

The dog looks up at me, then promptly lies down at Lou's feet.

I call the puppy a few more times, but he's not budging. Finally, Lou pipes up, "He's okay here. You two go along now. The pup will be fine."

As Stewart and I walk toward the general store, I ask him if the dog will be in Lou's way.

Stewart shakes his head. "No. My grandfather loves animals. He lost his old dog a year ago, a lab he had since it was a pup. He was devastated for a good couple of months. It's only lately that he's been talking about maybe getting another one."

"So, this may be a blessing in disguise."

"Exactly."

After I shop for tea, bread, cheese, and enough ingredients to make a hearty soup, Stewart insists on carrying the bags home for me.

We walk in silence for a while. Then I turn to Stewart. "I noticed people looking at us a bit funny while we were shopping together."

He bites back a smile. "Yeah, I haven't been seen with a girl before, so I'm sure they'll be gossiping for days about it."

I shake my head. "Folks can be so trivial. There were so many people in Vancouver, no one paid much attention to what others were doing. I must keep reminding myself that I'm not on the mainland anymore."

After Stewart helps me put the groceries away, I put water on the stove for tea. As we sit and talk, it occurs to me that having him to chat with is a godsend. Billy works twelve hours a day, and when I finally see him, he's too tired to engage in conversation.

Once the teapot is empty, Steward says he should be on his way. "Lou might need help in the shop."

I thank him again for his help, then follow him to the door. As Stewart descends the steps, the wagon carrying the miners pulls up.

A wave of anxiety rushes over me. I'm not ready for Billy to meet my new friend. My brother has always been overprotective when I'm around men, and I don't want him to embarrass me. I assumed I'd have time to bring up Stewart later to get Billy used to the idea, but no such luck.

When Billy sees Stewart walking down the stairs, he does a double take at the cabin number, obviously thinking he's at the wrong cabin. I step onto the top stair. "Billy, this is my new friend, Stewart. And this is my brother, Billy."

Stewart extends a hand for Billy to shake. Billy doesn't take it. "I'm filthy."

With nothing else said, the men pass on the stairs. After Billy enters the cabin, I tell Stewart I'll see him later and close the door.

Billy drops his bag on the kitchen floor, then sits at the table.

"Don't you want to look at your room before eating? And what about washing up? I still have some warm water left over from tea that I could—"

"No. I'm tired and famished. I'll wash up after I eat and see my room when I go to bed."

I sigh, then take out a jar of canned salmon and a loaf of bread. I begin arranging a plate.

"So, who's this Stewart?"

"I met him through the cobbler, Lou. Stewart is his grandson." I put the plate in front of Billy and sit across from him. "He's a very nice person. You'll like him once you get to know him."

Billy devours his food. In between bites, he continues talking. "You know better than to have men in your home while you're alone. What the hell were you thinking?"

I opt to keep my voice calm so as not to escalate things. "As I told you, Stewart is a nice person. I completely trust him."

"I swear, you must've left your brain back in Vancouver." He swallows a mouthful of bread. "What do you think the neighbors will say about you? We're not in the big city anymore, sister. Here, everyone knows what you're doing before you've done it. And what they don't know, they'll assume."

"Well, if the neighbors can't keep their eyes and opinions out of my business, I don't want to know them, anyway."

Billy shakes his head. "I've got enough on my shoulders. I don't want to be defending your name in the process. I don't want this Stewart person in this cabin when the two of you are alone, and that's final."

"Excuse me, brother. But I am not your child. I am a grown woman and don't need you to govern me." My temperature—and volume—start to rise.

Much to my surprise, instead of matching my growing anger, he takes a deep breath and puts his hand on mine. "I just want us to do well here or anywhere. I know that I'm not your father. I never wanted to assume that role. I'm sorry if I upset you. You are a very bright and strong young lady now. I am trying to protect you because you're my little sister, and I care."

My anger disappears. "That was unexpected. Was that an apology, big brother? Quick, get me a pen. I've got to write this down."

He shrugs. "Maybe working in the mines has tamed my fiery temper."

I laugh. "I'll say. Next, you'll want to borrow one of my dresses."

"Nah. I've seen your wardrobe."

When he's cleaned his plate, I pick it up, then offer to make him tea.

He shakes his head and gets up. "I'm just going to clean up and hit the hay. I'm sure looking forward to my day off tomorrow."

Suddenly, I remember the poster in the hotel lobby. "Billy. There's a play showing downtown tomorrow evening. I don't know how much it costs, but will you take me if we have enough money? It would be good for us to get out and do something fun together."

Billy's tired eyes meet mine. "I'm sorry, sis. It's my only day off. I don't want to get all dressed up and sit in a crowded room for hours. If your heart is set on going, I can give you a few dollars."

I sigh. "I guess I understand."

Billy heads to his bedroom but stops in the doorway. He glances over his shoulder. "I like the cabin. Whatever you did to it, you did well. Which is more than I can say about the dinner you prepared."

"You're funny. I'm sure the soot on your hands didn't help the flavour."

"Can you bring me a warm bowl of water with a bar of soap and a cloth, please?"

Only if I can dump it over your head.

Then it occurs to me. I forgot to buy soap and cringe as I fill the bowl, making a mental note to pick up whatever I overlooked in town tomorrow.

Chapter 4

My eyes catch the light as it shines through my bedroom window and illuminates the room. Almost immediately, my thoughts go to the play and the fact that I have no one to accompany me tonight.

I don't want to change Billy's mind. He's been working long hours at a challenging job that's new to him. No matter how badly I'd love him to go, I can't be selfish and push the issue.

But I still don't want to go alone...

* * *

Stewart arrives on time in Lou's carriage. When I open the door, I'm surprised to see his disheveled red hair tamed and styled. He's wearing a grey suit with a white collared shirt and polished black shoes. He looks like a true gentleman.

"My, you look smart, Stewart."

The compliment makes him blush and look away. "You look very nice as well."

After a bracing ride in the winter evening air, we reach the theatre. On the wall of the building is a large poster: *The Grand Duchess Starring British Actress and Vocalist, Marjorie Green*.

Looking around, I'm shocked at the overwhelming turnout. Every attending couple is dressed in the finest of clothing for the event. I hear a familiar voice chatting behind us, and when I turn around, I see my soon-to-be boss, Betty, holding a little girl's hand. When our eyes meet, she waves, and I wave back.

Once the doors open, it takes quite a while for the line of people to file into the theatre. Once inside, Stewart and I search for empty seats in the crowded room. Then Stewart taps my shoulder and points to two empty chairs halfway down the theatre. After we sit, I look around. The stage has long, red draped fabric loops above the closed curtains, and the orchestra is on the floor facing the stage, arranged in a horseshoe.

The delight of being here makes my skin tingle. I am transported back to those nights at the theatre with my mother. There's the same excitement now as I had then—the thrill and anticipation right before the curtain rises.

I look over at Stewart. "Thank you for coming with me."

He grins and is about to say something when the lights dim, and the orchestra starts to play.

The curtain slowly rises. I lean forward in my seat as the set is revealed.

At center stage is a green velvet sofa with two high-back chairs on either side. Hanging on the back wall are large, framed portraits of royal figures.

The scene soon erupts with half a dozen men darting out from either side of the stage. They wear dashing red military suits adorned with gold corded epaulets on the shoulders and shiny metal buttons down the front. The actors form a line at the front of the stage, singing. When the song finishes, the men quickly exit, and the orchestra begins a pleasant and uplifting melody.

The first thing that enters is the bottom of her brilliant red dress. She gracefully makes her way into the light at centre stage—she is breathtaking, one of the most beautiful women I've ever seen. Her shiny auburn hair is pulled back into a low bun, a sparkling tiara rests on her head, and her glossy red lips perfectly match the color of her dress.

However, her looks are only secondary to her voice. When she sings, the entire room grows silent in awe of her magnificent talent.

Each scene is better than the next, with bursts of dancing, powerful music, and just the right amount of humour to captivate the audience. After the final bows and the curtain falls, I feel saddened that it's over, but also fortunate I attended such an incredible show.

* * *

On the way home, Stewart and I talk about the show, with particular attention paid to the star, Marjorie Green, and her magnificent performance.

I look up at the night sky. "I wish my mother could have been here tonight. She would've loved it."

As we continue toward home, Steward tells me that Lou has come up with the perfect name for the pup.

"What is it?"

"Sparky."

"That's a strange name for a dog. Why did he name him that?"

"He said that when he was cleaning out the coal ashes from the stove, the dog was nearby, and an ember caught the fur on the end of his tail. Ever since then, Grandfather calls him Sparky."

I smile. "Lou is such a character. I hope the puppy didn't get burned."

Stewart shakes his head. "No. It just singed his fur."

I say good night to Stewart, then quietly walk into the cabin, knowing that Billy has probably gone to bed already. After tiptoeing into my room, I'm just about to close my door when I look across the dark hallway and notice that Billy's door is open.

Billy always closes his bedroom door.

A strange fear rises inside me. I creep across the floor, then stand at the entrance of his room and whisper into the darkness, "Are you okay?"

No answer.

Suddenly, my stomach clenches, and my hands tremble. This time, I call out louder. "Billy. Are you all right?"

Still, there's no answer.

Now my stomach is in my throat as I slowly step into the room and walk toward his bed. When I feel the mattress bump my leg, I bend down and reach my hand out to touch my brother. I run my hand over the width of the cot, but there's no one here. I sigh with momentary relief until I remember him telling me he needed to be in bed early to get a decent sleep before his shift.

I'm instantly mad. Where the heck is he? It's not like we have friends in Cumberland that he could've visited. My mind goes immediately to the pub in town. All I can do is pray he's not there.

I walk out to the front room and light the lantern, then sit at the table to wait.

Hours pass, and my eyes grow heavy. I do my best not to nod off, but I'm slowly losing the battle to stay awake.

I know there's nothing I can do to make Billy appear. Regardless if I'm sitting here at the table or lying in my bed, he's not coming home any sooner.

* * *

It's still dark out when the front door shutting echoes throughout the cabin and wakes me. Sliding out of my bed, I hurry into the cold front room, where Billy is taking his coat off.

"Where were you? You had me worried to death."

When he looks at me, and I see his eyes, a wave of relief hits me. He hasn't been drinking. Still, with his furrowed brows, it's obvious he's upset about something.

"Go to bed, Heather. That's where I'm headed."

I place my hands on my hips and hold my ground. "I need to know where you were all this time."

"Didn't we speak recently about how I don't need you to parent me?"

"Yes. But there's no way my nerves can handle any more of your disappearing acts. It drove our mother crazy with worry, waiting for you to come home all night. And guess who waited up with her?"

Billy unties his dirty boots and kicks them off. "I'm taking the day off tomorrow. We can discuss it then. I've had a bad night, and I'm in no mood to hash things out with you right now."

"No. Not this time. Tell me where you went. Did you go to the pub? Is that where you've been? You might as well come clean with me, Billy. I'm not going to let you get any sleep until you talk."

Billy slams his shoulders back and puffs out his chest, as when Mother pushed him to confess.

"Fine." His tone is beyond irritated. "I was gambling. There you have it. Now, I am going to bed—"

"Gambling?" My eyes instantly well up with tears. "How could you?"

"I don't need a guilt trip right now, Heather. I made a mistake, and that's it. End of discussion."

"Didn't you learn anything from your past mistakes? And now here we are, alone in a strange place, and you decide to fall back into bad habits." Tears stream down my cheeks.

"I said that I made a mistake. It's not like I planned it."

"I think you did. That was the reason you didn't want to go to the play with me. You were planning to go out and gamble."

"That's not true. Days ago, one of the men on my crew told me about a place in Chinatown where he goes to play cards. I went there to see him, not to gamble."

"Don't lie to me. I may be younger than you, but I'm no fool. I've watched you spin out of control too many times, and it always started with a bad decision. You can't do this again. You're all I have. This time when you self-destruct, you'll be taking me down with you."

He grows quiet and looks away. "It was one game. I lost, and now it's over. End of story."

"End of story? I wish I could believe that. How much did you lose? You never did tell me how much we had when we left Vancouver. I gave you my measly savings, and you were skint broke before Mother died. Where did you get all the money to travel here, then stay in hotels and sustain us?"

"Just forget it."

"No. I want the truth."

"It doesn't matter now. Whatever I had leftover is gone, so I don't see the point in talking about it anymore."

Suddenly, something awful occurs to me. I gasp, and my head starts to spin. I walk over and sit at the table. "Billy, where is our mother's gold wedding band?" I force myself to ask, though I don't think I can bear to hear the answer.

He sighs loudly, walks over, and sits across from me. He doesn't need to say a word. I look into his eyes and see the grim truth.

"How could you?"

* * *

93

The dark, rumbling sky mirrors my mood as I stand motionless at the window. Thankfully Billy is still sleeping, so I have some time to reflect. If we were back home in Vancouver, I would walk along the sea or find a park bench to watch the birds until I calmed down after an argument. Here, I have no idea where to find some peace.

Not wanting to wake him, I quietly walk to the stove, light it, and put water on for tea. I sit at the table with my hot cup, and memories of my mother float through my mind.

She was such a strong force that kept everything balanced in my life. Now that she's gone, nothing really makes sense anymore. I feel directionless and more alone than ever. The only thing Billy and I had to remember her by was the small gold ring my father had given her on their wedding day. She always wore it, except for the rare occasions when she would take it off for polishing. After she died, the hospital handed us a bag containing the clothes she was wearing, her worn shoes, and the gold ring. Now, Billy has sold the one meaningful token we had to remember her by.

When I hear Billy move around, I quickly rinse my cup and return to my room. I'm not ready to face him yet.

Billy is in the front room, and by the sound of clanking pots, I presume he's making something to eat. As I lie on my bed, I write a letter to Faye.

I write that Cumberland is a great place with kind and welcoming residents. I leave out the bits about the miners, the strikes, and anything else negative. I mention how I went to a play and briefly describe the most impressive moments. I'm about to stuff the completed letter into an envelope when I hear a soft knock on my door.

"Heather, I made you some breakfast. It's on the table."

"I'm not hungry."

"Come on. I went to the trouble of making it for you."

More so than not wanting to hurt his feelings, which I care very little about right now, I do not want to waste food, especially now that we don't have a penny to our name. Reluctantly, I leave my room and take a seat at the table. In front of me is a plate of beans and bread.

Billy sits across from me, and neither of us says anything for a while. Then after he swallows the last bite of his bread, he moves his plate aside and rests his elbows on the table. "Heather, I know you're disappointed with me. I'm disappointed with myself. But I need to clear the air about a couple of things."

I don't reply.

"I won't insult you by making excuses anymore. The truth about why I gambled last night is that I knew our funds were low, and I thought, just maybe, I could win a couple of hands of cards and double our cash. That is the honest truth. As for Mom's ring, I make no apologies for what I did. She died suddenly. I wasn't prepared. You weren't working full-time and couldn't make it on your own, so I needed to step up. I wasn't prepared for that, either. So, I sold the ring to Elsie, the widow who lived down the hall."

"Mom loved her."

"Yes. And Elsie loved Mom, too. She felt so bad when she heard that our mother had died. I showed her the ring, and she offered to buy it. After I sold it to her, she said that if ever we wanted it back, she would gladly sell it back for what she paid." He lets out a sigh. "I know you're upset. It made me sick to part with it, too. However, we were desperate. Again, I make no apologies for that. And I think our mom would agree with me."

I let his words sink in. "So, when we get enough money, we can get the ring back?"

"Absolutely."

My body starts to unclench as I realize Billy didn't really have a choice. And at least he didn't sell the ring to a perfect stranger. I'm so relieved that Elsie has it in her safekeeping. "I guess I can live with that. But, as far as the gambling goes—"

"You'll never have to worry about that again."

"I hope not."

He exhales, then grins. "So, what should we do today?"

"Why didn't you go to work?"

He shakes his head. "I need another day off. You have no idea what it's like. The strikers, the police yelling back and forth, people screaming at us, calling us every name you can imagine. Then there's the job itself. I never called myself claustrophobic, but since working in the mine, those dark, confining tunnels get to me. I admire the men who have done this job for years. Honestly, I don't know how much longer I'll be able to stick it out."

"But what will you do for employment?"

"Don't worry. I promise to keep at it until I secure another job."

I nod. "I guess it's good I start work in a week and a half. I'm not sure what the job entails or how many trips I'll be doing, but at least I can contribute something."

"See? Everything is going to work out."

"Except for now, we cannot buy more food or supplies. We're skint broke until you get a paycheck."

"I think we'll be all right. One of my crewmates said we could run a tab at most of the shops in town. At least we won't go hungry." Billy smiles, then adds, "By the way, I already know you're a terrible cook, but you should have paid more attention to what Mom bought when shopping. The items you chose were very interesting, to say the least."

"Is that right? Well, the next time you tell me to go shopping for food, you can forget it." I glare at him. "And what do you mean I can't cook? I cook just fine!"

"I'm not sure where you got that idea. Why do you think our mother did all of the cooking?"

"I don't know. I assumed she preferred it that way."

He shakes his head with a devilish grin. "She preferred not to get food poisoning."

I laugh. "It's a good thing you're so brave because guess who I'm going to hone my cooking skills on?"

"I hope one of our neighbors has medical training."

All is forgiven, and no ill feelings remain. Once our breakfast dishes are cleaned, Billy suggests we go for a walk to get *better-quality* groceries. Apparently, my interesting choices of food were less than desirable to him.

As we walk, Billy talks about how he's been thinking about moving us to Victoria because of its beauty and thriving economy. "I'll keep my ears open for employment opportunities there."

I remind him that we need to save money first, and the only way that's happening is if he behaves himself. He tells me how bossy I am, then suggests I consider a career as a schoolteacher. I agree, stating that I'm getting plenty of experience dealing with his childishness.

The gusting wind carries a sharp chill as we make our way up Dunsmuir Avenue. I quickly stop at the post office to mail my letter to Faye before we continue to the shops.

Billy's time in Cumberland so far has been occupied by the coal mine, so every shop and building is new to him. Before we get our groceries, I convince Billy to come to Lyster's Shoe Repair to meet Lou.

When the door swings open, Sparky, the pup, is on full alert and runs over to bark at the intruders. Lou says a few quick orders, and the dog promptly turns and trots to his side.

Billy shakes Lou's hand, and the three of us have a quick conversation before Billy suggests we get going. Before we leave, I think about asking Lou where Stewart is, but I quickly change my mind. Billy would accuse me of being in love and tease me all the way home.

On our way to buy food, we walk past the weaver's shop and see Shirley through the window. "She's very pretty," remarks Billy.

"She's nice, too. Do you want to meet her?"

"No. I'm all scruffy right now. Another time."

As we continue on, I see Betty walking toward us, carrying two large paint cans. When we approach, she sets the heavy cans down.

"Hello, Betty. This is my brother, Billy."

Billy grins. "You must be the crazy lass that hired my sister."

I fake a laugh, cringing inside.

Betty looks at me. "I guess it's just over a week before you start."

"Yes. I can't wait. It will be nice doing something productive to occupy my time."

"Cooking classes would've been productive as well," Billy says. But the joke is lost on Betty, who tells us she needs to get going, then picks up her cans and walks on.

As soon as she's out of earshot, Billy gives me a shocked look. "Was that really a lady? I mean, did you see her size? I swear, when you introduced us, I didn't know if I should kiss her hand or slap her on the back."

"Stop it, Billy. That's not very nice."

"I'm not trying to be mean. I just can't believe how broad her shoulders were—"

"Will you stop, please?"

Billy grins. "In all seriousness, I'm glad I met her."

"Oh, why is that?"

"Because as long as your working with her, I won't be worried."

"I don't understand."

"Let's say you two are delivering parcels with a buggy. If the horse gets tired, you can always hook up the harness to Betty, and she can pull for a while."

"You're not funny."

"I'm sorry. Just one more thing, and I'll shut up."

"What?"

"You may not want to get into an argument with her."

"Duly noted. Now, shut up!"

After setting up an account at the store, Billy loads canned meat, dried apples, raisins, bread, cheese, potatoes, carrots, and eggs into a basket, then arranges for milk to be delivered to the cabin twice a week. After watching him shop, I can see where I went wrong before. Mother always did the shopping, genuinely gifted at stretching a dollar. I should have paid closer attention. I'm nineteen and should know how to shop and cook, for that matter. Until now, my interests were in other things, like walking on the beach, window shopping, and meeting new people.

Billy and I tote our bags and take a long way home, walking across Derwent, Mayport, and Windermere Avenues, all roads I hadn't explored until now. Cumberland is a lot bigger than I thought it was. I make a mental note to spend more time getting familiarized with new shops and meeting more of the locals.

* * *

By the time we reach home, my feet are killing me and all I want to do is lie down on my bed. Billy is in a generous mood, telling me to go relax while he puts the tea on and makes us a snack.

As soon as I spread across my mattress, Billy walks in and throws something on my bed. I sit up and look. It's a copy of *The Iron Woman* by Margaret Deland.

"You didn't see me grab that, did you?"

A flood of warmth hits me. I shake my head. "No. But thank you."

As much as Billy stresses me out and gets under my skin, I love my brother with all my heart. I hope he can find a new job soon, which doesn't cause him as much stress as the coal mine. I just want him to be happy.

Chapter 5

The next week goes by in a flash. Billy works long hours, coming home filthy and exhausted, then going straight to bed, only to repeat the process the next day. I've been reading a lot, trying new recipes, and keeping everything in order at home.

Tomorrow is my first day at work. Although it will be nice to venture out, I have to admit that I'm nervous.

With chores done, I lay my clothes on the bed for work tomorrow, and then there's a knock at the front door.

To my surprise, it's Stewart, a letter in hand. I invite him in, even though Billy asked me not to be alone in the cabin with any male. He came all this way, and if I go outside to speak to him instead of inviting him inside, I know he will be hurt.

Once inside, he hands me the envelope. "I checked your mail for you. Thought I'd deliver it since I've meant to stop by anyway."

"How have you been?" I take the letter. After seeing that it's from Faye, I place it on the table.

"All right. Mostly, I've been helping my grandfather in his shop. He hasn't been feeling so great lately, so I try and pick up the slack."

"Oh no. I hope it's nothing serious?"

"He's had a condition in his lungs for a long time. He was advised to work less, but that news fell on deaf ears. To quote him: *You've got to pick yourself up by your bootstraps and carry on.*"

Stewart asks what I've been up to, and recounting my uneventful last week doesn't take long. "However, I'm starting work tomorrow and looking forward to doing things outside the cabin."

We sit at the table for the next hour while Stewart fills me in on any news he's heard lately. He updates me on the strikes and the robberies still occurring along the coast.

"Do you think they'll ever find the people responsible?"

Stewart shrugs. "I hope so. People are getting pretty fed up with the police for not catching the criminals. It says in the paper that the thieves aren't sticking to merely businesses and shops—they're also stealing food and supply deliveries dropped off at the wharves."

"That's terrible. I hope they're caught before someone gets hurt or killed."

"Well, a postmaster living on the Seattle coast was robbed and killed not long before the burglaries started here. Some think that incident connects to the rash of crime on BC's coast."

"I wonder if it's one person or a whole gang involved."

"There have been no eyewitnesses, so no one knows for sure."

We talk for a while longer, and somehow Chinatown comes up. I ask Stewart if he would take me there on one of my days off. "I'd love to look around. There's a large Chinatown just off Main Street in Vancouver." I tell him how my mother would take me there to buy all sorts of fabulous fresh produce when I was young. "I loved going there, if for no other reason than to breathe in the wonderful aroma of spices and food cooking in the streets."

"I think you'll like ours. There are more interesting shops than you can shake a stick at. It's a great place to grab a bite to eat, too. Though, certain residents in Cumberland aren't very keen on the place."

"Why is that?"

"Because of the gaming houses. To some church-going folks, gambling is a sin."

"Well, I'm not a regular churchgoer. Still, I tend to agree with them on some level. I'm not sure if gambling is a sin, but it definitely can ruin lives." I don't tell him what made me come to this conclusion. I'd rather not discuss it.

Stewart says it's about time he heads back to the shoe shop. I tell him I'll stop by to say hello if I have time after work tomorrow.

I watch him walk down the front steps and head up the road. I like him but not sure in what way…I think mostly as a friend. All I know for sure is I feel very at ease with him like I've known him forever.

* * *

After a fair attempt at dinner and no complaints from Billy about the meal, we both go to bed early. Billy, I'm sure, was asleep when his head hit the pillow, whereas I lay in bed and read Faye's letter.

She tells me how her little girl, Eva, is learning so much daily and about Charlie's long hours supervising the coke ovens. Then she writes about a terrible tragedy that recently happened in Union Bay. A well-liked Japanese man was killed when a landslide washed his home into the ocean. Finally, she asks if Billy and I like Cumberland and if we have met any friends yet. *Remember, Heather,* she writes at the bottom of the last page, *you're always welcome here.*

* * *

The acrid odor of stale coffee permeates the air when I open my bedroom door. Across the hall, Billy's bed is unmade.

I make myself a tea and take a few sips, then head back to my room to get dressed for my first day on the job. As I'm fixing my hair, the nerves start setting in. Despite my clenched stomach, I force myself to eat a piece of bread with jelly. Something tells me I will need all the energy I can get.

Outside the sky is clear, and my walk to town is relatively pleasant, besides the cool temperature. When I arrive at the shop, I see Shirley through the window setting up her rugs. As soon as I walk in, she looks up and smiles. "All ready for your first day of torture?"

I laugh. "I guess so."

Betty is sorting papers when I open the door and timidly enter the small office. She looks briefly at me, then goes back to separating pages. "Good morning. Are you ready to get to work?"

"I am. Yes."

"We only have one load today, with a quick stop in Royston, so we shouldn't be gone for too many hours."

"I'm at your disposal."

Betty grabs some papers, shrugs on her coat, and then we head out the front door. We walk to the back, where a medium-sized black workhorse is hooked to a cart with a front bench seat.

Betty gestures to the buggy. "I got the wagon ready this morning because it's your first day. Usually, we'll have to go to the

107

stables first to fetch the horse and buggy." She climbs onto the buggy, then motions for me to do the same. "We've got a load to pick up at the blacksmith's here, then deliver it to the blacksmith in Headquarters. It's a small town on the Tsolum River near Courtenay."

We trek along, crossing two streets before Betty pulls up at a large shop on the corner. She gets off the buggy and motions for me to follow.

I look up and read the artistic sign framed with gothic-shaped metal—*Alan's Blacksmith*.

A wave of hot air billows out of the shop the minute Betty swings the door open. When we walk in, a large man with a barrel chest and broad shoulders sets down a heavy-looking tool and approaches us. "Betty, how's everything going?"

"Okay. I've got a new worker learning the ropes."

"I'm Alan." He shakes my hand. "It's a big job you're signing up for. You should put some more meat on those bones." His face is warm and kind, and although I would normally take offense to a reference about my lankiness, I can tell that Alan means no harm.

"Whatcha got for me today?" Betty asks.

"Hand tools, barrel brackets, and some shovels." He walks over, grabs an armful of the heaviest-looking items, and then heads outside to the cart. Betty and I follow suit, with me taking the shovels and a few of the lighter tools.

"How are your animals?" Betty asks him as they load the cart.

I glance at Alan. "What kind of animals do you have?"

"Two horses and four donkeys." He laughs. "And they're all bossy females."

Once we've loaded the wagon, we say goodbye to Alan and head out. After leaving the downtown core, the road becomes bumpier, causing the tools in the back to clank and slide into each other.

I look behind us into the cart. "I hope nothing falls out."

Betty shakes her head. "Everything will settle."

I gaze at the tall, majestic trees passing by. "It's so beautiful here. You sure don't see such lush forests back in Vancouver."

"Yeah, I've been there. Not my kind of place. Too busy."

I ask how long Betty has lived in Cumberland. She tells me that besides spending six months in a fishing village up north, she's lived in the area all her life.

"Are you and Shirley old friends? Is that why you share the same shop?"

"Pretty much."

"That's great. It must be nice working out of the same space. There's always someone to talk to."

"Shirl is great, but sometimes she confuses me with all that talk about weaving." Betty rolls her eyes. "Her work is incredible, but why the hell do I want to hear about how she makes it all? I swear, if I have to listen to any more about beaters, weavers, or heddles, I'm going to fire that machine straight out the window."

I turn my head so she can't hear me giggle. I wonder what irks Shirley about Betty. From what I can tell, they are polar opposites. Shirley is dainty and soft-spoken, whereas Betty is broad and boisterous. I would love to be a fly on the wall of that shop when the two of them get into it.

Betty asks about the kind of work I did in Vancouver. She's not surprised when I list off jobs that don't require a lot of manual labor.

"Alan was right. You'll need to grow some muscle when you start working this job alone." Betty nods. "That being said, there's usually a man around to help load the cart, but you can't always rely on that."

* * *

The Tsolum River is noisy, raging, and spectacular. We ride alongside it as the white water rushes wildly past.

Up ahead along the banks, I see the small town. I want to ask Betty questions, but the roar of the river would surely drown out my voice. My eyes fixate on the blended colors of the immense maple, Douglas fir, and red cedar trees.

When we pull into Headquarters and up to the blacksmith's shop, Betty tells me to stay with the cart while she goes inside. Though Cumberland is far bigger than this town, there seem to be far more people bustling about.

After a while, Betty comes out and tells me it's time to unload the cart. Then she grabs an armload and takes it inside. Two young males walk by just as I climb down from my seat.

One stops and gives me a hand for balance as the other man looks into the cart. "Can we help you unload?"

I'm afraid to accept their offer. I don't want Betty to think I'm incapable of managing alone. I'm just about to refuse when Betty returns. "Why are you just standing here?"

"These nice men stopped and offered to help. I was just about to tell them that we can handle it and—"

"Don't be foolish. If they wanna help, let them. Until you build up your strength, accept all the help you can get."

With the assistance of the two, it takes no time to unload. When we finish, Betty offers to pay them. They both decline and tip their hats at us before walking away.

"You're lucky. You're a pretty young thing. I never took that into account when I hired you. With how fast those men showed up to help you, you may have an easier time at this job than I thought."

Betty turns the cart around at the end of the street, and I glimpse a vast brown building. "What is that place?"

"The new sawmill. The town is a logging community. You'll have a lot of deliveries here for one thing or another. The locals are a great bunch."

"It certainly is beautiful in these parts." I feel sad when we veer from the river and head back onto the road leading out of town.

* * *

Log booms sprawl over the still bay in Royston. As we pull up to the general store, Betty tells me she must go inside to pick up a very important item, which will take a while.

She ties the horse to a hitching post out front. "You can come inside if you choose."

I notice a small dock down by the water. Instead of following Betty inside, I want to stretch my legs.

The wind is colder by the ocean, so I wrap my arms around myself as I stroll. When I step on the narrow pier, I see that some boards are cracked and broken. Hanging onto the wooden rail, I do my best to step on the sturdier slats.

At the bottom of the dock is a small platform with a few metal cleats where smaller craft can tie up. Looking out over the blue water, I take a deep breath and fill my lungs with clean, salty air. Finding room between the cleats, I sit down and run my fingers through the cold water, every so often glancing up to the entrance of the store in case Betty comes out.

I'm watching the small fish dart around the wooden pilings beneath the surface when a loud splash startles me. My head snaps up to look over the bay just as a giant fish lands in the water and disappears into the deep, ripples fanning out.

"That was a big one," a voice says from behind me.

I gasp and turn around to see a man smiling at me. He's thirtyish, handsome in a rugged way, with a shadow of stubble on his face and eyes as blue as a sunny day.

"You scared me." I quickly get to my feet.

He laughs. "It's good to be scared sometimes, don't you think? It reminds us we're still alive."

"I didn't hear you come down the dock."

"I'm not surprised. I'm known for my ability to show up undetected."

I nod, not knowing how to respond.

"You're not from around here, are you?"

"No."

"I didn't think so. I would've remembered seeing someone as pretty as you."

I thank him for the compliment, then tell him I'd better get going.

"Why? Do you have to meet your husband?"

I shake my head. "No. I'm not married."

"Your sweetheart, then?"

"I don't have one of those, either."

"What about a big over-protective brother who will break my neck if he sees you talking to me?"

I smile. "Yes, but he's working."

"Then we're free to talk, right?"

"Actually, my boss is in the store. I should get back there in case she comes out."

"What is it you do?"

"I'm a courier. Well, sort of. I'm training for the job. Today is my first day."

"And do you like it so far?"

"I guess so. I mean, it's a job."

He takes a step closer, making me feel anxious and insecure. "A beauty like you shouldn't have to work. You should have a man to care for you and spoil you."

I laugh. "That's not the way my life is playing out so far."

Again, he steps closer to me, and my hands tremble. "And what's your name?"

"Heather."

He reaches out and takes one of my hands, slowly raises it to his mouth, and presses his lips against my skin. "I'm Henry."

I nod, then pull my hand back. "It's nice to meet you, Henry, but I should really be going now."

"I didn't mean to scare you away."

I shake my head. "You didn't. It's that I'm technically still working. I just came down here to get some fresh air."

He stares deeply into my eyes. For the first time in my life, I feel an overwhelming attraction to a perfect stranger.

"Well then." His voice softens. "I guess you'd best be on your way."

I smile then slowly edge past him. As I hurry up the ramp, he calls out, "I hope I see you again, beautiful."

His words are highly inappropriate, but for some reason, I'm thrilled. I know nothing about this man. He could be an absolute charlatan, propositioning women wherever he goes.

Or worse, he could be dangerous. There was definitely an element of wildness in those remarkable eyes.

Whatever the case, and whoever he is, I've never felt this intense energy before toward a man.

I reach the top of the pier just as Betty comes out of the store, carrying a small bag. "Are you ready to go?"

I nod. "Are we loading the cart first?"

"Nope. I've got what I came for." She holds up the small bag.

After we are seated in the buggy, I ask her what the important cargo is. She grins, then opens the sack and pulls out a piece of colorful candy. She shows it to me before popping it into her mouth. "This is the only place I can get my special saltwater taffy."

I laugh and shake my head.

As she turns the cart around, I see Henry standing on the pier. He's looking at me with a half smile. I quickly smile back, then turn my eyes forward. I don't want Betty to catch me flirting.

* * *

A cool wind follows us back to town, but for some reason, it doesn't bother me. I'm too focussed on my brief interlude with Charming Henry.

After the horse is unharnessed and back in its shelter, Betty shows me where the feed and water are before we return to the shop. Betty pushes the door open just as Shirley approaches. "I thought you two would've been back here long ago." She looks agitated.

Betty levels a gaze at her. "What's the problem?"

"One of the cross beams on my loom busted right in the middle of an order I was working on."

"What's a cross beam?" I ask.

Betty rolls her eyes. "Please, for the love of God, do not ask her about that damn machine. We'll be here for hours."

"Excuse me!" Shirley puts her hands on her narrow waist. "I've had just about enough of your sarcasm. I deserve more respect around here. After all, it's my business that keeps this shop running, and that includes that pigsty hovel you call an office."

"See you tomorrow, Betty." I slowly back out of the door.

Just as I'm pulling the door closed, I hear Shirley say, "Furthermore, we're inundated with mice. I'll bet anything you have food in your room, don't you?"

I'm smiling as I make my way to Lyster's Shoe Repair, thinking about the argument I just witnessed. For how ladylike and petite Shirley is compared to the masculine and brawny Betty, Shirley sure held her own.

* * *

Lou sits on a chair in front of the shop with Sparky faithfully curled up at his feet when I approach.

"How are you, Lou? I thought I'd come by to say hello to you and Stewart."

"Stewart is busy helping his neighbor with livestock. I don't expect to see him for the rest of the day. How was your first day as a courier? Stewart mentioned yesterday that you'd be working for Betty today."

"It was definitely a new experience, but I'm glad to be out of the cabin and seeing new places."

Lou asks where we made deliveries to, and when I mention Headquarters, he gives me some fascinating history about the place. Then he goes on about how well Sparky is settling in with him and how the dog gifts him with rocks whenever they walk. After half an hour, I tell Lou I must go home to make supper before Billy gets off work. "Say hi to Stewart for me. I'll try to stop by again tomorrow to say hello."

As I walk down the street, the local shop owners outside cleaning the front of their shops all smile or give a quick wave when they see me. It's not something that happens in the big city. Here, it seems that once folks get used to seeing you around, they go out of their way to be friendly.

When I pass all the shops and reach the winding dirt road heading for the cabins, I look at the houses with their picket fences and, for the first time since being here, feel a sense of home.

Chapter 6

The cold evening air rattles the windows of the small cabin. It's long past when Billy usually gets home from the mine.

I've prepared a nice little stew, which I'm keeping warm on the stove, and set the table with two bowls, bread, and butter. I'm about to get a sweater from my room when the front door opens, and Billy walks in.

As soon as I see the expression on his face, I can tell something is wrong. "Billy, what's the matter?"

He shakes his head. "Rough day. One of the men got hurt."

"That's awful. How did it happen?"

Billy sighs as he takes off his boots. "He got his leg slammed between two carts."

"Oh no. Will he be all right?"

"He'll live, but I'm sure he'll lose the leg."

"Did you see it happen?" I didn't need to ask. By the look on his face, I can tell he witnessed more than he'd wanted.

"Unfortunately, yes. He was standing mere feet from me when it happened."

"I'm so sorry, Billy. What a thing to have happened, and what a thing to have witnessed."

Billy washes up and gets changed while I fill the bowls with stew. He comes back in and sits down with a sigh. "You know what, Heather? I can't wait to quit this job and put as many miles between me and that mine as possible."

"I know. Have you heard about any other jobs?"

"No. But a few of the crew mentioned quitting so they could apply to the logging camps. That mine isn't safe. I feel lucky to be alive every day that I make it through another shift."

"I understand it's unsafe but don't accidents occasionally happen at most labour jobs?"

Billy glares at me. "You don't know what it's like, Heather. I've never felt this anxious going to a job before. I can't escape it. At night, I dream about bad things happening."

We eat the rest of our meal in silence. As I'm preparing to stand and clear our plates, Billy sits up straight. "Hey. I forgot to ask about your first day at work. How was it?"

I tell him about the beautiful Tsolum River and our trip to Headquarters, then mention our brief stop in Royston. However, I omit the part about meeting the unexpected stranger, Henry.

"The river sounds interesting." He stands with a grunt. "Maybe you can take me there on one of my days off." Billy stretches his back and then pats me on the head. "Dinner was great, sis. Tell whomever you got to make it that I really enjoyed it." He lumbers off to bed.

After cleaning up the dishes, I retire to my room and lie on my bed. As I listen to the wind rattling the windows, I think about my brother and how unaccustomed he is to working at a job as tough as mining. Billy is a city boy, born and raised. Neither one of us realized what hard labour truly meant.

Then, as my eyes grow heavier, my thoughts drift back to the dock, where I first heard Henry's soft voice behind me. I replay the interaction in my mind again and again. The last word I hear before falling asleep is Henry calling me beautiful.

* * *

Light snowflakes sweep my cheeks as the old nag pulls the cart down the road. It's the second trip I've made alone this week, and both have been to Royston.

Two days ago, I picked up a half dozen cases of canned fish and a thick bag of saltwater taffy for Betty. Before I went into the store to get the items, I had hitched up the horse and cart and walked to the small dock hoping to see Henry. To my disappointment, he wasn't there.

With each mile I travel toward the same location today, I have a growing doubt that once again, he won't be there.

By the time I reach the Royston store, my lap is wet where snowflakes have landed and melted. I tie up the horse with fingers frozen and stiff. While I want to walk down to the wharf before I pick up my load, I know it's too cold and decide to warm up in the store first.

Today, I've come to pick up milk, eggs, and potatoes sent from Denman Island, and are bound for the smaller grocery stores in Cumberland. The owner's wife, Claire, makes me tea while I sit at a small table, holding my hands next to their warm stove. It takes about twenty minutes before I'm reenergized and ready to load the cart.

Claire bundles up in a warm coat and gloves to help me load the wagon. When everything is packed up and secured, she slides off her gloves and hands them to me. "Use these until you get back to Cumberland, then buy your own. You'll be needing them. My daughter Maggie works at The Rusty Wheel Saloon, you can drop my gloves off when you've finished with them."

I'm embarrassed accepting the gloves on loan, but at least my hands will keep warm. I can worry about my pride later. Billy doesn't get his first paycheck for a few more days, so I haven't been able to upgrade my wardrobe to accommodate the new snowfall.

After Claire says her goodbyes and goes back into the store, I don't unhitch the horse immediately. Instead, I walk to the top of the dock and look down the long ramp to the platform at the bottom. I sigh in disappointment when there is no sign of Henry.

As I head back to the store, it occurs how silly I was to think I would see him. I have no idea who he is or what he does for a living. And the odds of him being on the dock by himself are slim to none.

Logically, my brief meeting with Henry was just a one-time thing. I'll most likely never set eyes on him again. I've got to stop obsessing over a stranger and get on with my life.

My spirits low, I head back to Cumberland, barely taking in the beauty of the freshly fallen snow around me.

* * *

I scarcely recognize the small room when I open the door to Betty's office. The tall stacks of papers usually balanced on her desk are nowhere, and all the dishes with dried food are gone. There is a small painted table in the corner which, due to clutter, I'd never seen.

Betty is sweeping with her back to the door when I step in.

"My goodness." I look around in awe. "Do I have the right office? It looks incredible in here."

She turns and looks at me. "Yes. But don't let Shirley know. I don't want her to think that all of her bitching and bellyaching about the mess is what prompted me to clean up."

I giggle. "Your secret is safe with me."

Betty helps me unload the cart outside, then tells me I have one more delivery tomorrow to Union Bay, then a few days off. As much as I want to work—God knows Billy, and I need the money—I'm looking forward to spending time in the warm cabin.

When I walk past Lou's shop on the way to deliver the gloves to Claire's daughter, I look in the window and see Lou working away with his back toward me. I'm relieved he doesn't see me. I'm in no mood to sit and talk after not seeing Henry.

I'm just about to step off the sidewalk onto the road when I hear my name. I turn to see Stewart standing in front of his grandfather's shop.

He walks to me. "How are you?"

I force a grin. "I'm fine. And you?"

"Good. I thought I'd walk you home to get caught up."

"All right. I have a quick stop before heading to the cabin." As much as I'm not in

124

the mood for company, I haven't seen Stewart in a while. After he's been so good to me, I don't want to seem rude by refusing his offer. Plus, I've never been to The Rusty Wheel Saloon before, and Stewart knows the town like the back of his hand.

I don't say much while he leads me across two streets and up to a tall, narrow white building with a large wagon wheel fixed above the entrance. On the door is a small wooden sign etched with the words—*The Rusty Wheel.*

I stand at the door, turn to Stewart, and then pull the gloves out of my coat pocket. "I need to drop these off for a lady named Maggie. However, now that I'm here, I don't think it would be appropriate to go inside alone. Would you—"

"You stay here. I'll go in and deliver them." He takes the gloves from me.

"Please tell her they're from her mother, Claire."

I wait in the cold for what seems like forever before Stewart finally reappears. "Sorry. I had to help Maggie with a small shipment of bottles."

"That's fine." I rub my hands together. "Did you give her the gloves?"

"Yes. Maggie said to thank you."

On the walk home, he tells me about Maggie, who came to the area five years ago to be closer to her mother. "Initially, Maggie wasn't the most popular among the women folk in town."

"Why not?" I hope some gossip will take my mind off how cold I am.

Stewart shrugs. "I guess they were a bit intimidated by her. She was—and still is—very attractive, and she was single when she first came here, so she turned a lot of heads. But it wasn't just her appearance that put her on the women's taboo list. She had also lived an unconventional life before arriving in Cumberland."

"Sounds intriguing. Tell me more."

"Well, from what I was told, Maggie was a cook in a logging camp in the interior. She probably heard and saw it all, exposed to many rough characters. Her experience in the camp gave her an edge the women here found intimidating."

"Do you mean that she spoke crudely and was abrasive?"

"No. Quite the opposite. Maggie's the sweetest of people, but when push comes to shove, and someone falls out of line in the saloon, she has no problem setting them straight."

"And for that, she was shunned?"

"Initially, yes. It's unusual for a woman to be so outspoken. But she's been here long enough now that the women got to know and respect her free-spirited character. Also, Maggie got married, so the women weren't as threatened."

"She married a local?"

"No. From California, I think. A man named Harpo sailed to BC from south of the border."

"And what is his story?"

"A saloon keeper, I've heard. Which makes him a perfect match for Maggie."

"That's nice, but it would have been a far more interesting story if he was a gunslinger or suspected notorious gang member who fled here seeking refuge."

Stewart laughs. "You should write books. We don't need any more outlaws here. From the news around town, the burglars hitting the coastal towns are still at large and continuing their crime spree."

"It amazes me that they haven't been nabbed yet."

"They will be. Their luck can't last forever."

* * *

When we reach the cabin steps, Stewart pauses. "Heather. I was going to ask you something." He looks suddenly nervous.

"What is it?"

He directs his eyes to the ground, reminding me of the painfully shy young man I first met.

"What is it, Stewart? Spit it out."

"There's a dance at the Union Bay Hall in a couple of days. There will be music and refreshments, and I thought maybe if you weren't busy…"

"Are you asking me on a date?"

"Well…"

"I'd love to go to a dance, Stewart. But in two days Billy will be off work. I don't feel right leaving him alone to twiddle his thumbs."

He nods solemnly. "I understand."

"Unless you wouldn't mind if he came along?"

He finally looks up. "Of course, I wouldn't mind."

"Then it's a date." I gesture inside. "Did you want to come in for tea?"

Stewart declines, telling me he must return to his grandfather.

I thank him for helping me deliver Maggie's gloves and for walking me home, adding that I'll try to stop by and see him at Lou's when I get off work tomorrow.

As I fill the kettle, I think about Stewart and what a kind, gentle man he is. I could have gone alone with him to the dance, but I'm not sure how deep my affections run for him and don't want to mislead him. Having my brother with us will make the evening less intimate.

Regardless of my true feelings for Stewart, I don't want to lose his friendship. He has a heart of gold and the very best character. However, he's not the man I met on the dock. If only I could meet someone who made me feel like Henry did.

* * *

Despite the cold and the newly fallen snow, Billy is in much better spirits than the evening before. I make thick sandwiches, and we sit down at the table. Billy asks about my day, and we discuss the weather. Considering how upset he was about working in the mines last night, I don't ask him how his shift went today. I wait until he's nearly done with his dinner before I broach the next subject. "There's a dance in Union Bay this Saturday. You're not working, so I wondered if you'd like to accompany Stewart and me." I brace myself for his rejection.

"Stewart?"

"Yes. He's asked me on a sort-of date, and I thought I could get you to come along so he doesn't get the wrong idea."

"You're agreeing to go on a date with him, but you don't like him?"

"I do like him. I'm just not sure in what way yet. As it stands, I'd prefer to keep things on a friendship level."

Much to my surprise, Billy shrugs and says, "I need a change of scenery. I'll go with you. Heck, you never know. Maybe I'll hook me a pretty young lady while we're there."

"Gee. I wouldn't go to the dance with that objective if I were you. You'll be setting yourself up for disappointment."

"Why is that?"

"Because I'm pretty sure the only woman who could stand you would be hard of hearing and have poor vision."

"You're a real laugh." He flings a chunk of bread at me. "You better treat me nicely, or I'll tell your Prince Charming just how much you pine over him every day."

"You'd better not. Just remember who cooks your meals every day."

Billy points to the sandwich crust on his plate. "I'm not sure if you're aware of this, but a sandwich is not supper food." He shakes his head. "I hope whomever you marry understands your lack of kitchen skills."

"That's why tomorrow, I'm making a special dish reflecting my feelings for you—pigs' head soup with chicken livers."

* * *

When I get to the shop, Shirley shows me her newly fixed machine just as Betty leaves her office. She seems hurried and tells me she'd already hooked up the cart and has everything ready for my day. She hands me a piece of paper to take to Alan, the blacksmith and tells me I only have one delivery to make in Union Bay.

The ground is frozen with a light dusting of snow, but the sun is out. Hopefully, the weather will be agreeable for my relatively short journey.

I head around the back of the building, climb onto the buggy, and head to the blacksmiths.

Alan walks out of the back room just as I enter the shop. He smiles. "Good morning. Not quite finished with the tools going to Union Bay as I've got one axe that needs a handle yet. Shouldn't take more than a few minutes."

I pull a chair up close to the tall table he's working at. "Have you always lived in Cumberland?"

Alan laughs. "It feels like it, but no. I moved out here from Killam, Alberta, about twenty years ago."

"I've never heard of Killam. Is it a big place?"

He shakes his head. "If you blinked, you'd miss it. Mostly just homesteads there."

I ask if he had come west with his family. He says that he and his father traveled out together in 1893.

"My goodness. That was a long time ago. I wasn't even born yet. I bet it was much harder to travel on the roads back then."

Alan laughs. "A bit bumpier in spots. But otherwise, pretty much the same."

"So, is your father here in Cumberland with you?"

He smirks. "You ask a lot of questions, don't you?"

"Yeah. I guess I do. My mother used to say that I never had the good sense to know when to stop talking."

Alan shrugs. "That's all right. I don't mind. And yes, my father was here with me for a few years, but then he passed away."

"I'm so sorry. I hope I haven't opened an old wound."

"It's been a long while now. I've come to accept it."

"So, you're alone now?"

"All but me and my mules and horses, yes. But when I crave socializing, I meet the locals and have a few beers."

"That's good." I smile. "I don't know many townspeople other than Lou, the cobbler, and his grandson, Stewart."

"Well, you picked a couple of the best. Lou is a salt-of-the-earth character, and his grandson is a replica. Lou has done most of the raising of that boy, and he turned out well. If Stewart is the only friend you make here, you've done exceptional."

"Yes. He seems like a sincere young man. I've been enjoying the time I've spent with him."

"As for Lou, don't get caught in a crib game with him. He's older than dirt and has learned to play that game like a pro. Just last night, he took me for four bits."

I laugh. "I'll keep that in mind."

Alan finishes attaching the handle to the axe and then gets the tools together for the delivery. I help load the cart, and it's ready to go in no time.

When Alan hands me a slip of paper to give to the shop owner in Union Bay, he looks down at my proffered hand. "Do you not have gloves?"

Embarrassed, I shake my head. "I just haven't gotten around to buying any yet."

Alan sighs and then tells me to wait while he runs back inside. A few moments later, he returns with a medium-sized pair of gloves. "Here. Wear these. They'll be big on you, but at least your hands won't freeze."

"Are you sure?"

"Of course. These belonged to a young man who used to work for me. He left them here, so you might as well put them to good use."

* * *

A light blanket of white covers the trees as the cart ambles along the frozen ground, the only noise I hear is the crunching of snow from the wheels and the horse's hooves. I breathe in and fill my lungs with clean winter air. It's so pretty here. I wish my mother were still alive to see it. She would have loved the area.

Other than passing the odd buggy, my trip is solitary and serene. It doesn't take long before I'm approaching the first row of cabins in Union Bay.

I maneuver along the main road, avoiding carriages as I navigate to the small shop near the train station, where I'm to deliver the tools.

When I arrive, I tie the horse to a hitching post and go inside the small, dirty shop with scraps of metal and pieces of wood stacked on shelves. An elderly man wearing a heavy apron is reads a book in the corner of the room.

I pull the piece of paper that Alan gave me out of my pocket. "Excuse me, sir. I am here to deliver the tools you ordered from the blacksmith in Cumberland."

He remains fixated on his book for a few more moments, then, without making eye contact, tells me that he'll call his son to unload the cart, but it will take a while. I place the paper on the nearest shelf and tell him I'll wait outside.

I pet the horse and watch people make their way to and from the train platform. The last train I took was when Billy and I boarded together after spending the night at Cousin Faye's. I should make a point of stopping in at her house to see her, but I know she'll want me to come in and have something to eat. Then we'll start talking and lose track of time. My worse fear is travelling back to Cumberland in the dark. I've seen the odd posters around town warning people about the mountain lion and bear sightings. With the old mare pulling the cart, we couldn't outrun a raccoon, let alone a hungry predator.

Feeling the cold, I'm just about to go back into the shop when I hear my name in a soft, husky voice. I turn and look behind me.

Across the street, walking in my direction is Henry.

Immediately a shiver runs through me. I can't believe he's here. He's been on my mind so much lately. I've daydreamed about running into him, but I never thought I'd see him again, let alone here in Union Bay.

My stomach fills with butterflies, and my hands sweat despite the cold when he reaches me.

He stands in front of me and smiles that same handsome grin. "Hello, beautiful. What are you doing here?"

My eyes fall to the ground. "I was going to ask you the same thing."

"I'm working. And you?"

I motion to the cart behind me. "I'm delivering tools."

"Are you waiting for them to jump out of the cart and walk into the shop themselves?"

I laugh. "No. I'm waiting for the shop owner's son to help me unload. Some of the items are very heavy."

Henry nods. "I'll tell you what. I'll help you unload your cart, but you must come for a soda water with me."

"Where?"

"There's this little shack by the beach I sometimes hide in to get away from my workers."

"Your workers?"

Henry nods. "Yes. I have my own construction company. That's why I travel from place to place. There's always someone needing a house built or repair jobs done."

"That's great you have your own company."

"It has its moments. So, what's it going to be, Heather? Do we have a deal?"

"I really shouldn't, but it will be okay if we're not gone too long."

"Shall we?" He smiles, then walks over to the cart and picks up a large, heavy sledgehammer in one hand, and several axes with the other. He waits for me to grab what I can out of the cart.

After a few quick trips with Henry packing hefty loads, the cart is empty, and we're riding across the road to the beach. Henry points out a narrow pathway that runs through a clearing. There's no way the horse and buggy will fit without damaging the cart, so Henry gets down and leads the horse to a post at the side of a small restaurant. He asks me to wait, then goes inside and buys two bottles of soda water.

Henry takes my hand to prevent me from falling as we trudge along the bumpy pathway.

He was right; the small building couldn't be described as anything but a shack. The tiny room is nothing more than four walls and a little window. Bits of paper litter the floor, and the only places to sit are a feeble little stool or a dried-out stump matching in size.

I step inside. "My gosh. This room has seen better days."

Henry opens the sodas and passes me one. "As I said, it's just a place to come, have a cigar, and be alone with my thoughts. What about you, Heather? Do you have a little hide-a-way to escape to?"

"I don't, and I don't need one. I live with my brother, who works all day, so I'm mostly alone."

"Cumberland, huh? Let me guess. Your brother is a miner?"

I nod.

"That racket ain't for me. They couldn't pay me enough to work in one of those dark pits. I've known a lot of men who have mined. Every one of them aged about ten years in six months. That's why I started my own company. I decide where I'm going and set my own prices."

"Do you live in Union Bay or Royston?"

"Neither." He walks over to the window and points out at the water. "Look over there, to the tip of Denman Island."

I walk over and gaze out the window.

"That's where I live."

"So you travel back and forth each day?"

He shakes his head. "Not always. Sometimes if I have to work early in the morning, I'll stay in Union Bay. But the days I finish work early, I jump into the boat I keep at a small dock not far from here and go home."

I nod. "What's the bay where you live called?"

"Henry Bay."

"You're kidding. Did you name it after yourself?" I giggle.

"No. But whoever did name it had good taste." He winks.

I keep gazing at the tip of the beautiful little island. "I'd love to visit there."

Henry steps up behind me, so close that I can feel the warmth of his breath on my neck. "*Love looks not with the eyes, but with the mind; and therefore, is winged Cupid painted blind.*"

His words cover me with tingles, making my head feel light and woozy. "Where is that from?" I don't turn.

"Shakespeare."

"You know Shakespeare?"

"Some. My uncle came over from England when I was in my teens. He brought books with him. I read that line all those years ago and haven't thought of it again until now."

I take a deep breath and muster my courage, then turn and look him in the eyes. "That was a beautiful thing you said to me. Thank you."

He leans forward and gently kisses my forehead. "If you lived here, I could easily fall in love with you."

"But you don't even know me."

"I know something special in you makes me want to know more. Both times I've seen you, I feel such a strong connection. Don't you feel it too?"

I drop my gaze. "Yes."

"Then we owe it to ourselves to explore that feeling."

"What do you mean?"

His fingers gently guide my chin upward until our eyes connect. "I mean that, for whatever reason, we crossed paths. It's like destiny. And maybe I'll never meet anyone again that makes me feel the way I do when I look at you. And the same could be said for you. What if you never feel this connection with anyone ever again? Wouldn't you regret not giving us a chance?"

"But what are you suggesting, Henry?"

"Let's spend time together. Become close friends. Let fate take care of the rest." He smiles, and his crystal blue eyes light up the room.

We stand in silence, looking out the window at the beach. Henry stands close to me, and I feel the energy from his body on my skin.

My brother would be horrified by the idea of me standing in this little shack with a man I barely know. A part of me knows that the intimate words he said are inappropriate, considering we're not well acquainted in the slightest. But the other part of me is completely beguiled. And I want more.

He steps away from me. "We should be going. You need to get that horse and wagon back to Cumberland, and I need to supervise my men."

"You're right. If I don't make it back to my boss's shop, she'll wonder what happened to me."

He takes my empty soda bottle and places it with his on the windowsill, then grasps my hand, leads me out of the shack, and back onto the path. Walking behind him, I ask if he's free tomorrow evening. "My brother, my friend Stewart, and I are going to a dance here in Union Bay."

"I'd love to, Heather. But I'll be working in Courtenay on a barn repair job. I won't be finished there for a couple of days."

"That's too bad. I would've liked to introduce you to my brother."

Henry stops and turns to face me. "If I ask you to meet me here at the shack in two days at around noon, will you come?"

I tell him I will, even though I cannot get to Union Bay without deliveries. I don't want him to lose interest. Besides, I have two days to solve the ride issue.

Henry quickly kisses my hand when we arrive at the horse and cart. "I'll see you soon, beautiful."

* * *

I'm halfway through the journey back to Cumberland before I realize I've been daydreaming about Henry without paying attention to the road. Fortunately, the horse has traveled this route many times and knows the way home.

Henry is more than I could ever hope, intelligent and passionate, proving that when he quoted Shakespeare. He also has a strength that I haven't seen before in any man. He wasn't afraid to share his true feelings with me.

Granted, I was a bit taken aback by the nature of his comments. I was raised to believe that men should be subtle with a lady until they become better acquainted. Henry doesn't fit into that mould. Instead, he is a free thinker, like a poet.

Betty is cleaning the small stable when I arrive. "How was your trip?"

"Everything went smoothly."

"Your brother came by the shop about an hour ago. I told him you were on a delivery in Union Bay."

"My brother? But he's supposed to be working. He wasn't injured, was he?"

"Didn't look hurt to me. I saw him head over to the post office. He seemed just fine. I wouldn't worry yourself."

I quickly help unlatch the cart from the horse, then tell Betty I'll see her tomorrow before hurrying out. Instead of stopping in to say hello to Lou and Stewart, I head home immediately.

* * *

I'm not sure if it was from the brisk walking or the biting cold air in my lungs, but I'm panting and out of breath by the time I reach the cabin steps. I hang onto the railing and steady my breathing before walking up the steps and opening the door.

The smell of freshly brewed coffee hits me when I walk in. Billy is sitting at the table, playing solitaire.

"Why are you home? Are you all right?" I'm still struggling to take a full breath.

"Of course." He doesn't look at me.

"I heard you went by Betty's office today looking for me."

"I was in town and thought maybe I'd catch you at work."

"I went to Union Bay. Will you tell me why you're not still at the mine?"

"Just a few hours after I arrived this morning, rocks and debris started to fall in the pit. They told us to come up to the surface until they secured things. Since I got paid today anyway, I thought the time off was a good opportunity to go into town and settle our food tabs."

I sit down to take off my boots. "You must have gotten home not long after I left this morning. Did you return home immediately after stopping in town?"

"After I was done paying the bills and ran out of money."

"Out of money?" I join him at the table. "But you've only just been paid. I don't understand."

Billy takes his eyes off the cards and looks at me, irritated. "I had gotten an advance about a week ago, so I didn't receive a full paycheck today."

"An advance for what?"

"Just forget it, Heather. It's none of your business."

I shake my head. "You borrowed money against your pay when you went gambling before, didn't you? It wasn't just the money you had left in the pockets that you bet with—you borrowed more." My face is suddenly hot.

"That's not what happened. Besides, you're not the one working in that hell-pit mine every day, so you should have no comment on what I do with my pay."

"Wrong. We both have jobs so that we can get ahead. We'll never save a penny if you're borrowing toward your paycheck."

"Then it's a good thing we still have your pay coming in."

"Yes, except you forgot one thing, Billy. We have to survive until I get paid. I don't understand you." I stand and head to my room.

"Don't you want dinner? I'm about to start cooking."

"No. I haven't much of an appetite right now."

It's hopeless. I don't know why I ever thought he could change from who he was growing up. He will always be this way, struggling for money and being irresponsible. As long as I live with him, I'll be anxious about his actions and if the bills get paid.

I change out of my dress and into looser-fitting clothes, then lie on my bed. I'm so frustrated with Billy that I can scream, but instead, a tear trickles from the corner of my eye.

When he confessed to gambling, why did he still lie? Why tell me he'd only spent what was on him? Now I'll always wonder if he's taking advances to gamble. I won't believe a word he says.

There's a soft knock on my door. "Heather. Would you please stop catastrophizing? We're going to be just fine. I won't borrow any money toward my paycheck again. I promise."

"I don't want to talk to you right now. You lied to me."

"You're wrong. And you'll feel bad when I prove that to you."

"Go away!" I holler.

Billy opens the door a sliver. As soon as I see his face, I grab my pillow and whip it at him. The pillow misses the door and hits the wall, and something falls out of the pillowcase. I sit up just as Billy opens the door wide.

"What did you drop?" he asks.

I get up, walk over to a tiny box on the floor, and pick it up. "Where did this come from?" I examine it.

"I don't know. Open it." To my surprise, Billy is grinning.

I walk over to the bed, sit down, and take the lid off the box. I can barely believe what I'm seeing. It's our mother's gold wedding band.

I take it out of the box and slide it onto my finger. Tears flow like rain.

Billy sits next to me and puts his arm around my shoulders. "I never lied, sis. I got an advance so I could send for the ring."

I turn to him and wrap my arms around his neck. "I love you, Billy. Thank you so much. I'm so sorry I accused you of being dishonest."

He pats me on the back. "I know how much it means to you. And maybe now you'll believe me when I say that I'm not gambling. My plan is to save my next paycheck, so you and I can get away from here—from the mine, the strike—and move to Victoria."

"Did you get a line on a job there?" I hope he hasn't. I don't want to move that far away from Henry. I'd never see him.

"Sort of. I heard about positions working on the railway. It's probably not my dream job either, but at least it's above ground."

"Maybe there's a job around these parts. Victoria is such a long way away."

Billy looks at me with suspicion. "What's up with you?"

"Nothing. It's just…I don't mind the area so much. And traveling to the south tip of the Island would be quite an undertaking. But we don't need to stay in Cumberland. Anywhere nearby—Royston or Union Bay—would be fine, if you get a job you like." I fiddle with the ring. "All I'm saying is one place is as good as the next, right?"

"I know you, Heather. You have a motive for wanting to stay around here."

"I most certainly do not. I like the people here in Cumberland. That's true. But I would be thrilled living in any town near here."

Henry smirks. "Okay, if you say so. I still think you're hiding something."

"That's because you've always been the king of secrets. And just because you're that way doesn't mean I am."

He doesn't respond, but I can tell by his expression that he knows something's up. "Heather, Victoria is a city. It's not as big as Vancouver, but it's bigger than here. You may feel more at home there."

"I feel at home just fine around here. Do you have clean clothes to wear at the dance tomorrow?"

"No. I thought I'd borrow something of yours."

I laugh. "There's an image I didn't need in my mind."

"What's wrong? Are you afraid of a little competition?"

"If you in a dress is competition for me, I might as well give up now."

* * *

Stewart arrives just as the last glow of the sun dips behind the trees. Billy looks as he used to before a night out in Vancouver, dapper in his black blazer and matching trousers. He's even managed to scrub most of the coal dust from the creases on his face, with only a fine line of black around his lashes, making his light blue eyes more striking.

Stewart wears a black blazer as well, though the fit is boxier and the arms longer than if the garment had been custom-made for him. His trousers are ones I've seen him wear before, with even a tiny stain on the knee. Still, his attempt at dressing up is appreciated, and I pay him a compliment that immediately causes him to blush. As for me, I finally have an excuse to wear my pinstriped dress with a high lace neck that I've kept neatly tucked away for a special occasion.

Thankfully, Lou was gracious enough to let Stewart take his horse and buggy to the dance, which I will most definitely thank him for the next time I see him.

* * *

Billy stands on the dance floor with one of the more attractive ladies. When the band starts up an upbeat ragtime tune, my brother begins to dance, or his interpretation of dancing. It looks more like a cat that got its head stuck in a tin can.

I cover my mouth, not wanting to laugh out loud, then turn my attention to Stewart, unable to bear the spectacle. Stewart turns from my brother to me. "You never told me that Billy was a modern dancer."

"Didn't I? Well, he is. The dance he's doing now is called *The Electrocution*."

"Do you want to dance? Or are you too afraid of getting hit by Billy's limbs?" Stewart laughs.

I giggle. I'm delightfully surprised by Stewart's sarcasm. He'll fit in just fine around Billy and me. "I don't think I'll do much better than Billy. I've not been to many dances."

"I love to dance. For some reason, when the music starts to play, and my body starts to move, all of my shyness kind of drifts away."

I spot a group of ladies huddled in a corner of the room. They are in bright, colorful dresses and are smiling and talking. "Look, Stewart. There are four attractive gals that look agreeable. I'm sure at least one of them would be happy to dance with you."

Stewart shakes his head. "It's okay, Heather. I understand if you don't want to dance, but I came here with you, and I'm not about to ask anyone else to dance with me."

I sigh. "All right. I'll dance with you, but don't blame me if I step on your feet."

He smiles. "Don't worry. I'll lead you."

We wait for the song to end, then I reluctantly follow Stewart to the dance floor. I look over to see Billy's dance partner leaving the floor. Billy returns my gaze, shrugs his shoulders, and, with a laugh, walks off in the opposite direction.

The band begins to play. Right away I recognize the song: "Let Me Call You Sweetheart," one of my favorites. I look up at Stewart, then down at my feet.

As soon as he takes my hands and starts to move, I want to close my eyes and pretend no one can see me as I did as a child. I'm as stiff as a board when we do our first turn.

Stewart leans down and whispers into my ear, "You are the prettiest girl in the room, and you're dancing just fine. So relax."

As if his words are magic, my body relaxes, and my anxiety eases. Soon, Stewart and I are floating around the dance floor. By the time the song ends, I'm excited for the next tune.

As everyone claps for the band, I see Billy walking toward us. On his arm is a blond lady with an impeccable figure. When they get closer, I'm shocked to see that the woman is Shirley.

They make their way toward us, and I have just enough time to nod a quick hello before the next song starts. When Stewart and I take the first few steps, Billy spins Shirley around with such force that her shoe catches the back of my leg.

Her eyes are aghast. "I'm so sorry," she mouths.

I grin my forgiveness while grimacing in pain. Stewart quickly tries to dance us away from my brother-turned-court jester and his unlucky dance partner, but in no time, Billy is right beside us again, flailing like a headless chicken. And even though the music is quite loud, I hear the odd groan and protest as my brother swings Shirley around like a human weapon.

I'm more relieved than anything when the song ends. Apparently, Shirley feels the same way because she's beelining it off the dance floor.

Stewart offers to get me a soda water, then leaves me near a wall as he heads toward the bar at the other end of the building. I watch the couples on the dance floor, dressed in their fanciest attire. Everyone seems happy, and there's an excited energy humming in the air.

Billy walks over to me. His face is flushed, and he looks spent. "That was a lot of fun. I gave Shirley a run for her money. I bet she's never had a dance partner like me."

"That's safe to assume."

He glances around the room. "I wonder where she ran off. Have you seen her?"

"I don't know." I shrug, then continue under my breath, "She's probably gone in search of a crutch."

"What?"

"I said, I think she liked your dancing very much."

"Yeah, I like to take things up a notch when I'm out there. Sets me apart from the others."

"You're not kidding."

Stewart returns, and we drink our sodas while Billy is homing in on another dance partner. Then the two of us laugh until tears stream down our cheeks, watching Billy flail his newest victim around the floor.

Since Billy has work early the next morning, we only stay for a couple more hours before heading out. On the road back to Cumberland, Billy points out different constellations in the night sky. I refrain from cracking jokes about his awkward display on the dance floor—it would be too easy. Plus, he's happy right now. I don't want to tease him and burst his bubble.

At the cabin, Billy goes inside while I thank Stewart for taking us to the dance. We share a couple of quick laughs about my brother's wild interpretation of the tango, and I'm just about to say good night when he leans in for a kiss. Taken aback, I move my head to the side, avoiding his lips.

He pulls back quickly. "Oh. I'm sorry. I didn't mean to offend you. I thought—"

"I'm not offended, Stewart." I quickly think up an excuse. "It's just that my brother may be watching."

There's a moment of awkward silence before Stewart clears his throat and says he should be on his way.

I feel awful as I watch the buggy travel up the road. Stewart' feelings are stronger than mine, especially since I met Henry. I pray the embarrassment isn't still thick between us when I next stop by Lou's shop.

Chapter 7

Eerie moans from Billy's room force me out of a deep sleep. I grab my robe and pull it on as I hurry across the hall to his room. Slowly I open his door, then listen hard. If he moans again, I'll wake him from his nightmare. Otherwise, I'll let him sleep. He has to be up shortly, and after arriving home quite late last night, he needs all the rest he can get.

Thankfully, after a few more moments, I hear him breathing peacefully.

* * *

The wind roars over the thin windowpanes of the cabin. I wake a little late, so I quickly get dressed and head to the front room. I lace my shoes and pull on my coat without stopping to make food or even a cup of tea. On my way to the door, I notice a small piece of paper on the stove. It's a note from Billy.

I don't have time to read it, so I stuff it into my pocket and hurry out the door. The freezing wind burns my face as I walk briskly toward town. I look up and notice dark, angry clouds churning overhead. What a dreadful day. Even though Billy hates his job, I'm glad he's working below ground.

I wonder where I'll be making deliveries today, hopefully to Union Bay. As much as I'm not looking forward to braving this nasty wind, I'd love the chance to see Henry again.

The creaking of the entry door alerts Shirley, who sits on a stool in front of the loom. She turns and gives me a quick smile. "I hope you had a good time at the dance last night."

I look down at her ankles, half expecting to see a bruise from being flung about on the dance floor by Billy. "I had a wonderful time, thank you. It was nice to get out and have fun. How about you? Did you enjoy the dance?"

She giggles. "It was interesting."

I appreciate that she didn't mention my brother and how badly he must have embarrassed her. I walk past her and quickly knock on Betty's door before opening it.

There are two huge crates on the floor. Betty pops her head up from behind one of them. "Hello, Heather. I'm getting things ready for a delivery tomorrow. These crates are full of bedding and other linens that must be taken to Comox."

"You don't want them delivered today?"

She shakes her head. "The weather is too bad, and with the look of those clouds in the sky, I can't be sure if it's threatening rain or snow. Either way, a storm is coming. I don't want my horse or you venturing out in it."

I feel a wave of disappointment. I won't be able to meet Henry today, like I'd promised him. "I understand. You don't need me today, then?"

She shrugs. "There's always something to do around here if you want to work. You can grab a broom and go through this office and Shirley's shop too. After that, you can dust and tidy whatever needs tidying. You'll probably get a half day of work out of it."

I take off my coat and reach behind the door for the broom. A half day's pay is better than taking the day off and not making anything. And Henry would understand. With luck, I'll meet up with him tomorrow instead.

* * *

It's just after lunchtime when I've finished cleaning the floors and wiping down every surface. I'm glad when Betty tells me I can leave. My stomach is grumbling from not having time to eat breakfast.

I wish the ladies a good day and tell them I'll see them bright and early tomorrow, then head out. Usually, when I've finished work, I stop by Lou's to say a quick hello, but considering the ugly weather, I head toward home instead. Plus, I'd rather not face the potential awkwardness with Stewart quite yet.

Thankfully, the wind is at my back, making the walk home more bearable. I'm just nearing the edge of town when I see Alan, the blacksmith, coming up the road on his horse and buggy.

I smile and wave, but I see his serious expression as he gets closer.

He pulls alongside me and stops the buggy. "You'd better come with me."

"Why?"

"Your brother's been hurt. He's at the hospital. Climb on, and I'll take you there."

He grabs my hand and helps me into the buggy.

My immediate thought is there has been a mistake. "Are you sure it's Billy that's been hurt? How do you know?"

"I had to tend to some business up at the mine today. Just before I was set to leave, there was a commotion at the entrance. Four men were carrying a man who didn't look to be in very good shape."

"That's terrible, but that doesn't mean it was my brother."

"One of the men in charge asked if I knew the injured man's sister. *'They live together in one of the miner's cabins,'* he said."

I try to speak, but no words will come out. All I can do is stare at him.

In what feels like no time, we're pulling up to the hospital. Alan pats my leg a couple of times, then gets off the buggy and comes around to my side to help me down. I try to move quickly, but my bones feel heavy and make it hard.

Alan leads me by the hand as we walk to the front door, just as two miners are walking out. One is older, maybe in his sixties, whereas the other is around Billy's age. The older of the two has a sullen expression and frowns when he sees Alan.

"How's he doing?" Alan asks.

The man shakes his head, looks down, and continues walking.

Please, God. Please let my brother be okay. I can't do this. I can't.

We walk down a short hallway, at the end of which stands two nurses outside a room. They notice us, and one asks if we are here to see the young gentleman just brought in from the mine.

Alan nods, then motions to me. "This is his sister, Heather."

I point to the door. "Is my brother in there?"

One of the nurses nods. "I am so sorry."

"Why are you sorry?" A wave of panic rushes through me.

Instead of waiting for an answer, I push through the door and into the room.

There, on a cot, lies my brother.

He has a wrap on his head, blood seeping through, and his face is as grey as ash.

I slowly walk up to the side of the bed and notice his arm is covered in dried blood. I reach out and touch his limp hand. "Billy, please wake up. I need you to stay here with me. Please, Billy." A sob chokes me.

A nurse, I didn't hear come in, places a hand on my arm. "I know this must be hard for you. I'm terribly—"

I whirl around. "Where's the physician? He should be here. He should be trying to save him."

"We did all we could, dear. He is barely hanging on, and you need to prepare yourself."

"That's not true. If you did all you could, he'd be awake. Now, get the physician and fix my brother!"

The nurse's expression is full of sympathy. "The physician knows what he's doing, and he's seen these injuries before. Trust me, at this point, our hands are tied."

"He is young. He is strong. If you would just do as I ask and get the damn physician back in here—"

Alan appears and, with his big arms, grabs me and pulls me into his chest. "Try and calm yourself, Heather."

"I can't! I can't! Please, Alan, please tell them to wake Billy up."

As Alan holds me, a man in a long white coat and a stethoscope hanging over his neck walks into the room. His voice is soft but direct. "Your brother sustained blunt force trauma. It's my understanding that a large boulder broke loose from the ceiling in the mine pit and struck him in the head. Because of the severity of his injury, we have sedated him so it's easier on his body. Whatever happens with him now depends on how much fight he has left in him."

I push myself away from Alan and turn to look at my big brother.

Even when Billy came home drunk to the gills and passed out on our mother's sofa, there was still life on his face. But looking at him now, there's nothing there. He looks ashen and frozen.

I slowly walk to the side of the bed, lean down, and push my cheek against his. "Billy. I love you always. I'm sorry if I was a pain. And I hope, wherever you are right now, that you come back to me soon. I can't live without you."

I don't remember walking out of the hospital. All I can recall before I left is a nurse asking me to sign a form, then reminding me that I must prepare myself for the worst. I don't remember answering her or talking to anyone else on my way out of the hospital.

When Alan drops me off at the cabin, he asks if I have any relatives nearby. I tell him about Faye and Charlie in Union Bay. Then he leaves, and I'm alone in the cabin.

It isn't long before Stewart shows up. I don't answer the door, so he lets himself in and finds me curled up on my bed. I can't speak a word to him as he sits next to me and puts his hand on my shoulder. Slowly, I feel my mind slipping into a dark, terrifying place.

I'm not sure how many hours pass as I lie motionless on my bed. All I know is when I suddenly hear Faye's voice, it makes me cry harder.

There are other voices coming from behind her. I have no idea what they're saying, and I don't care. All I can think about is Billy and how I will truly be alone if he dies.

Faye sits on the bed beside me and slowly strokes my hair. "Heather, I've just come from the hospital. The doctor told me that Billy has been calling out, and he even moved his fingers. He said that Billy will be kept under sedation to make sure he stays calm, but considering the extent of his injuries, the doctor is very pleased and surprised by his sudden progress."

For the first time, I look up at her. "He's going to be okay?"

"We don't know the extent of his head injury yet. But so far, Billy's reactions are making the doctor hopeful."

I sit up and wrap my arms around her. "Thank you for coming here, Faye. And thank you for telling me about Billy."

Chapter 8

A couple of weeks later, Billy has improved tenfold. His motor skills are slow, and it takes him a while to try and explain things, but he's alive. I couldn't be more grateful. I walk up to the hospital every day to see him and stay as long as the nurses let me. He gets tired quickly, so I usually spend most of the visits sitting beside his bed and reading a book.

Yesterday, when I got home from the hospital, a man stood on our steps holding a clipboard. He told me that since Billy was no longer working at the mine, we would have to leave the cabin, as another family needed it. Thankfully, Stewart dropped by shortly after the man had left and offered to take me to talk with Faye about what to do.

Right away, she suggested that I stay with her until Billy gets better and is released from the hospital. She even offered to arrange for our belongings to be shipped on the train from Cumberland to Union Bay, where she would store everything for us.

The hardest part of moving away from Cumberland while Billy remains in the hospital is that I won't see him daily. That said, I need to focus on finding employment and a place for us to live. Not only that, but I'll need to find employment until Billy is well enough to work again.

* * *

The sun beams through the lace curtains and dances on the wall. I sit up and try to stretch. My body feels stiff and frail after meeting the train in Union Bay and, with the help of Stewart, unloading all of Billy's and my belongings.

Slowly, I slide out of bed and shuffle into the front room. The smell of bacon cooking and fresh coffee is good.

I head to the kitchen, where Faye is leaning over a pan on the stove, her back to me.

"Hi." My voice sounds raspy and tired.

Faye turns quickly, a smile lighting her face. "Heather! You're up."

She asks if I'm hungry, and when I nod, she tells me to have a seat at the table. She pours a coffee, fixes a small breakfast plate for me, then sits across the table. "You know, you can stay here as long as you like, Heather."

I take a sip of coffee. "I know. And I appreciate the offer, but I can't stay forever. This is your life, not mine. You have Eva and

Charlie to care for. You don't need me in your way."

"We're family. We can make it work."

I shake my head. "I need is to find a way to earn some money to set up for when Billy gets out of the hospital."

"I understand. You know, I did hear of a job opening at the little store here by the beach. Mr. Leung and his family own it. They're lovely people. If you like, I can take you there tomorrow to speak with them."

Although my tiredness has mostly lifted, I still feel a bit hazy, but time is ticking by, and I've got to take the first step toward my future. "Thank you, Faye. I'd appreciate that."

I help do dishes and tidy up, then Faye takes Eva for a short stroll on the beach. I go back to my room and sort through my clothing until I find something suitable to wear when I inquire about the job tomorrow. I'm straightening up my coat when I reach into the pocket and feel a small piece of paper. I pull it out. It's a note. The note Billy left for me on the morning before he got injured.

I sigh deeply and read his words:

Heather, I had a great time at the dance. Thank you for asking me to come along with you and Stewart. By the way, he's a good man. Maybe you should give him a chance. See you after work. Love, Billy.

A warm tear rolls down my cheek as I hold the letter to my chest.

I love you too, Billy. Always and forever.

After a while, I stuff the note back in my coat pocket. As much as reading it hurts me now, I know later it will give me strength.

I look out the window and watch Faye play with Eva. Soon, my focus shifts up the beach toward the shack where I was last with Henry.

Since Billy got hurt, I've thought of Henry very little. Now that I'm feeling a little better, I'm wondering if Henry still goes down to the old shack to escape things and smoke a cigar. And if he does, I wonder if I'm still in his thoughts or if he's forgotten all about me and moved on. I didn't honour our agreement. I didn't meet him at the shack, and he wouldn't have known why.

* * *

A little bell chimes overhead as Faye and I enter the Leungs' small store early the next morning. My stomach flutters with nerves.

There are three aisles with stocked shelves and a counter with a register at the back. As we walk farther inside, an older Chinese man appears in a doorway covered with a long, red curtain.

Faye introduces me, then asks if there's still an open position for a store clerk. Mr.

Leung's English is very good when he tells us he's still looking for the right person. Like a promoter, Faye lists my good qualities and attributes.

The man looks me up and down, then nods. "Okay. We will give it a try. She can start tomorrow."

We spend a few more minutes in the shop while Faye buys a couple of tins of tomatoes and a bag of candy for Charlie. Outside the store, I thank Faye for getting me the job, even though the butterflies have doubled in my stomach. I can only hope I'm able to fulfill the duties expected of me.

Faye senses my trepidation and laughs. "You think too much. I'm sure you'll do just fine."

As we head up the road toward Faye's, I hear my name. I look around, and across the street is old Lou on his horse and buggy, Stewart sitting beside him.

Excitement jolts through me, and I wave at them. Lou turns the buggy around and comes up alongside Faye and me.

I introduce the men to my cousin, then ask how they are doing. While Lou answers, Stewart's eyes search mine intently. It's like he's trying to read me, to gauge whether I'm doing all right.

After we talk for a few minutes, Faye sighs and looks at me. "We must be going. I need to spell off Charlie from watching Eva."

I nod, though I don't want to say goodbye to my friends just yet. Talking with them has made me feel more like myself than I've felt in weeks. And as though he can sense my feelings, Stewart pipes up, asking me if I'd like to join them for lunch.

Lou drives the buggy to the hotel, and we get a table at the restaurant there. Once we're seated, Stewart and Lou fill me in on what's been happening in Cumberland. From Betty hiring a new delivery person, a young man new to the area, to Shirley doing well with her rugs. "Oh, and Alan told me, if I saw you, to give you a big hello from him," Lou adds.

Thinking of Alan makes me think of the last time I'd seen him at the hospital and how caring and comforting he was while my brother's fate loomed over me. I push the thoughts from my mind and smile at Lou. "Tell Alan that I send a hello back."

We order sandwiches and talk between bites. Lou raves about his pup, Sparky, and I tell them about my new job starting tomorrow at Leung's grocery. The three of us talk until Lou checks the time on his pocket watch and says they should be going.

We walk to the carriage outside, and Lou offers me a ride home. I tell him that it's such a beautiful day, I prefer to walk. I give both Stewart and Lou the biggest hugs. "I hope to see you two again soon."

Stewart seats himself in the buggy and shoots me a grin. "I'm counting on it. I still owe you that trip to Chinatown, after all."

I watch as they ride down the road. I am so happy I got to see them both and grateful they didn't bring up Billy during our visit.

* * *

As soon as I walk in the door, Charlie and Faye tell me they have some news I may be interested in. Curious, I follow them into the front room, where I sit across from them on the sofa.

Charlie explains that the colliery businessmen that often come to town stay at a small cabin only ten minutes away. "It has two bedrooms and is right on the beach. It's vacant if you're interested."

Faye nods enthusiastically. "You've mentioned how you wanted to find a home for you and your brother quickly. Well, now that you have a job at Leung's, you'll be able to afford a place."

I beam at the two of them. "This is wonderful news. I can't thank you enough, Charlie."

Faye lays a hand on her husband's arm. "Because Charlie is a valued employee of the company and you're family, you'll only have to pay eight dollars a month."

"I don't know what to say. I never expected such good things to happen to me so quickly. I'm overwhelmed." I focus on Charlie. "But what happens when someone who works for the colliery comes to town? Will I need to move out while they're here?"

Charlie shakes his head. "The town's inn has agreed to keep a couple of rooms open. Since there's a restaurant and pub downstairs, it's far more convenient for the men to stay there."

Faye waves a hand. "Of course, you'll need to personalize the cabin. From what Charlie has told me, the inside is nothing fancy."

I'm now fighting tears, and I stand to hug them both. "Oh, I don't care how plain it is. I'm overjoyed I'll have a place of my own."

Charlie hugs me tightly back. "I'm glad you're happy. I can take you over there to look when you get off work tomorrow."

* * *

Mr. Leung is kind and patient as I learn the ropes of working in the store. My duties so far include stocking shelves, straightening cans and jars so the labels point outward, sweeping the storeroom, emptying mousetraps, and helping customers find items—mindless tasks I could have done when I was a child. It's okay, though, because the slow pace and low pressure of the job are just what I need right now. A stressful, fast-paced job wouldn't have been something my nerves could handle. Billy's injuries still hang over me, and I'm still wrought with fear about how well he will heal.

Mrs. Leung and her two children are quiet and disappear when customers enter the store. They live upstairs, and when there's no one shopping, I hear them walking and moving about.

When my shift ends, Mr. Leung tells me that I work well and he'll be happy to keep me as an employee.

Charlie is walking up to the door just as I leave the store. "Are you ready to see your new home?"

"I've thought of nothing else all day."

We walk down the road, passing small homes, the post office, and a restaurant before turning right and walking up a narrow road. There are large maple trees and red cedars on either side of us, and I imagine how beautiful the green leaves will look once spring arrives.

Charlie glances at me as we walk. "We'll be sad to see you go, Heather. Your staying with us has made Faye so happy."

He then briefly mentions Billy and how much of a shame it is for such a young person to have suffered such a tragic accident. "I'm so glad to be managing the coke ovens and not working in the mines. I couldn't muster the strength to toil long hours in a dark pit. I just don't think I could survive in that atmosphere."

"Billy used to say the same thing. That's why he was only going to work for another month. After that, he was planning to move us to Victoria." A hard lump forms in my throat. "He wasn't miner material, and he knew it. He couldn't bear that job. I only wish he could've gotten out of the mine before the accident happened."

Charlie touches my hand. "I know how close you two are, Heather. In time, Billy will be well again, and your lives will return to normal. You have to believe that."

"Thank you, Charlie. I need all of the positivity I can get right now."

* * *

The cabin is much as Charlie said it would be—plain and needs a personal touch. There is a large front room that looks out over the beautiful bay and two modest bedrooms, along with a kitchen and a pantry. Although there is furniture throughout the cabin, it doesn't feel warm or lived in. I'm going to make it a priority to change that.

Charlie gestures to the place. "So, what do you think?"

"It's perfect, Charlie. I can hardly wait to move in."

He studies me closely. "Are you going to be all right, being all alone here?"

"Oh yes. I'm looking forward to it."

Despite my confident tone, apprehension is creeping up on me. I haven't ever lived on my own before. I've been so excited about getting this cabin that the reality of being all by myself hadn't occurred to me until now, seeing these sparse, lonely rooms.

I've always lived with family and taken for granted the security of knowing someone else was in the house, especially at night.

Nerves begin bundling in my stomach. I walk over to the large windows overlooking the sea and take a few deep breaths.

I am going to be fine. This is what I need, a place where Billy can come home. And as for Cousin Faye, I've imposed on her family long enough. Besides, she's mere minutes away if I need anything, especially if I take the beach route. In the words of old Lou, I've got to buck up, pick myself up by my bootstraps, and carry on.

Chapter 9

White foam explodes high in the air as huge waves crash against the craggy rocks on the shore.

Thankfully, I'm less tired today. Over the past week, I've been kept awake during the night by the noises outside my cabin. I've gone to work tired and unfocused. Last night, I decided my exhaustion was too much to bear, and since the noises I've been hearing haven't led to anything threatening, I placed my pillow over my head and went to sleep.

Faye has stopped by a few times with linens and a couple of warm blankets, along with a box of spices and canned goods. Still, my work at the grocery has put me behind on laundry and housework. Thankfully today is my day off, so that I can get caught up. If I finish quickly, I can walk on the beach and maybe write a letter to Lou and Stewart.

* * *

A forceful wind makes the walk to the shoreline strenuous and slow. I find a log to sit on, then watch the white and grey gulls ride on currents of air overhead.

I spot a small craggy stick and pick it up, then drag it through the sand, bringing small rocks and empty clam shells to the surface. From the rhythm of the sea and nature, there's a peacefulness about this place that speaks to the deepest part of me. Even as a child, I felt more in touch with myself if I played near the ocean. Other children would tire after a long summer day at the beach, but not me. My mother would have to drag me away from the water.

After a couple of hours, pangs of hunger hit me, so I get up with a stretch. I'm starting the walk back to the cabin when, out of my peripheral view, I see someone strolling on the beach with a dog, heading this way. I seize the opportunity to meet one of the locals and walk toward them.

Once I'm closer, the elderly man nods a greeting. I bend down to pet his senior Irish Setter, and the man asks me where I'm from. I point toward the cabin. "I'm new to the area."

"I'm Luke Kingery. This is Red. My wife Annie and I moved up from the States quite a few years ago. We have a house not far from here."

The man is warm-natured and chatty. He asks where I originally came from and then talks about the community and how fond he and his wife are of the area. "Until all of the burglaries started happening," he finishes, shaking his head.

"I know. It's terrible. I presumed the criminals would've been caught by now, but no such luck."

Red starts barking at a gull and then beelines for the water. Luke yells after Red, and when the dog doesn't heed, he grumbles, "I'd best go after him. The silly mutt will dive in the water chasing birds, and he's liable to get caught in the current."

Instead of walking back the way I came, I keep strolling on the beach until I see a clear path leading to the road. That way, I can stop in at Leung's and buy an apple before going home.

A few minutes down the beach, I spot a clearing between two houses I can walk through. I am about to head toward the opening when I look to my left and see the small shack that Henry took me to. Suddenly, I have a strong desire to peek inside.

As soon as I pass the trees, I see the small front window where we both stood together and looked out at Denman Island. I grab the door handle when I hear scuffling from inside.

I quickly release it, then turn to hurry away when the door swings open.

I whirl around to see Henry with a cigar in his mouth. He looks at me somewhat perplexed before it dawns on him who I am.

He slowly takes the cigar out of his mouth. "What? Heather. What are you doing here?"

"I was just walking on the beach, and I saw the shack and thought—"

"Where have you been? I never thought I'd see you again."

"I know. I'm so sorry I didn't come back when I said I would. A lot happened, and I couldn't get away."

Henry shakes his head, then chuckles. "It doesn't matter now. You're here."

He throws his cigar onto the rocks, then steps to me and wraps his arms around my waist. "I'm so happy to see you. I had no idea where to start looking for you."

It feels so good in his arms. I melt into him.

We walk into the shack and sit down. I open up about Billy, my new job, and the cabin down the beach I'm renting.

He leans over and brushes my cheek with his hand. "I'm so sorry about your brother. Nothing can prepare you for that kind of devastation. But I'm happy you got a job and thrilled you have your own cabin. Maybe you can show it to me."

I nod. "Yes. Of course."

"How about now?"

"Now? But don't you have to get back to work?"

"I was just heading out to check on my men and make sure everyone knows what they must do. But I can be a bit late."

I ask him what he's been working on lately, and he tells me he's been building a barn in Courtenay for the last couple of weeks. I ask him another question, but instead of answering, he stands up and extends a hand toward me. I take it, and he pulls me up.

"I'm dying to see this cabin of yours. Will you show it to me?"

I smile and nod. "I'd love to."

Walking up the beach to my cabin goes a lot faster than the walk to the shack. I'm so excited to see Henry again.

At the cabin, I turn the handle and swing the door open. Henry follows me in and closes the door behind him, looking around with a slight smile on his face. "This is perfect."

"Do you think so? I haven't finished decorating yet."

He laughs. "Well, it's a lot better than that damn shack."

I take him on a quick tour of the place. Despite him following close behind me, I'm still hardly believing he's actually here.

Once we're back in the front room, he takes me by the hand, then pulls me close to him. This time, instead of kissing my forehead, he slowly presses his lips against mine.

Once I feel the warmth of his lips and the heat of his breath, my whole body fills with shivers. After a long kiss, he holds me tightly in his arms.

"Will you let me come and spend time with you here?" he whispers.

"Of course, but what about your home on Denman?"

He pulls back to meet my gaze and rests a hand on my cheek. "I'll spend every free minute I can with you."

I cover his hand with my own. "I'd like that very much. I'm usually finished at the store by five o'clock. I'm home shortly thereafter."

"I'll meet you here tomorrow." He lifts my hand to his mouth and kisses it. "Now, don't you be running off on me again."

I laugh. "There's nowhere else I want to be. Especially now."

"I'm glad to hear you say that. I'll see you soon, beautiful."

Henry walks to the door. Right before he opens it, he turns back. "There's only one problem. If I end up visiting too late, I may need to spend the night. It's hard to navigate my way home to Denman Island in the dark."

"Oh. Okay. I'm sure we can work something out. My cousin brought me an extra blanket, so..."

Henry winks. "Don't worry about that now. I'm sure we'll come up with a solution."

I don't take a full breath until he's gone. I'm in total disbelief.

I never imagined I would see him again. Now, not only is he not upset with me for standing him up, but he's more smitten with me than ever. I can't believe it. I feel like I'm on top of the world.

I spend the evening making sure the cabin is dusted and swept. Then I tear through my clothes, desperate to find a nice outfit for after I get off work tomorrow.

* * *

The morning sun shines down on the calm sea, creating the illusion of a million diamonds sparkling on the surface. I dress for my day of work and make a quick breakfast of bread and jam before heading out the door.

Customers are already browsing through the aisles when I arrive. Usually, when it's busy in the morning, the pace continues throughout the day, and I fall behind in cleaning and stocking. Thankfully, I have Henry to muse about throughout the day, so time passes quickly.

When my shift ends, Mrs. Leung meets me at the door and hands me a big container of homemade food. I thank her heartily but don't stop to chat; I need to be home with enough time to make myself presentable for Henry.

* * *

It's seven PM. I had spent considerable time making sure my hair was just right, applying enough powder on my cheeks, and dabbing on a hint of lip color before sitting on the sofa and gazing out the window into the night. Despite my time spent getting ready, I've been waiting for nearly an hour.

I worry that Henry has been delayed. However, I find it hard to imagine how he can do his job once the sun goes down.

As time ticks by, memories of my mother and Billy float into my thoughts. I twist the gold band around my finger as I think about them laughing and joking with one another. They used to fight like nobody's business, but they had the exact same sense of humour. Their relationship was an extreme one. If they weren't fighting about something, they were laughing their heads off. I smile and press the ring to my lips.

The clock hits nine PM before I decide Henry will likely not show up. Knowing that I work early tomorrow, I change into my night dress, then, with some sadness, unpin my hair and wash the powder and colour off my face. Disappointed and rejected, I go to bed.

* * *

A hard rapping shocks me out of my sleep, and I sit bolt-upright in bed. There's no way a tree branch tapping on the window or a critter on the deck could've caused that noise.

My heart's thumping as quickly as a rabbit's, I slide slowly out of bed and pad into the living room. The moon shines through the window, creating an eerie blue path on the floor I follow to the front of the cabin. My breaths are short into my constricted lungs as I tiptoe closer to the door. My gaze flicks past every window, trying to see movement or shapes, but there's only darkness.

Hand shaking, I reach out and take hold of the cold doorknob. I turn it in tiny increments, preparing for the door to burst open. Images of bears and cougars enter my mind. The area is known for these predators.

I set my jaw and decide that, if it's an animal, I'll yell and scream and clap my hands to scare it away.

The knob stops turning, and I cautiously ease the door open inch by slow inch. And my heart just about jumps out of my chest when I see Henry slouched forward on the front step.

I yank the door open fully. "Henry, what are you doing? Are you okay?"

He slowly lifts his head and smiles. "Hello, beautiful."

I exhale, and my tensed muscles relax. "Are you going to come in?"

Henry gets his feet under him, wobbling before regaining his balance. "Oops. I may have had a few too many drinks tonight."

When he passes me, a waft of liquor hits my nose. All I can think about is the hours I'd spent getting ready and waiting for him to come when he'd promised, and meanwhile, he'd chosen to get drunk.

However, I hold my tongue. I remember vividly the times Billy came home drunk, where I learned very quickly not to confront him. Alcohol is a fuel for arguments. Truth be told, I can't stand being around anyone who's drunk—even if that person is Henry.

I get a blanket and a pillow and pile them on the sofa. Henry flops down and pats the cushion beside him. "Come and sit next to me, beautiful."

"I will tomorrow. Right now, I have to get some rest. I work very early in the morning."

"Oh, come on. Just for a second?"

Reluctantly I sit beside him. Immediately, he puts his hand on my leg and leans in for a kiss, and the stench of booze is overwhelming. I pull my head back. "I'm sorry, Henry. But I really do have to get to bed."

He scoffs and pulls back. "So, you don't want to kiss me because I'm a little late? Need I remind you about how you stood me up? Did I get upset with you? Did I reject you?"

I stand up and look down at my drunken guest. "I'm sorry you're upset with me, Henry. I don't mean to make you feel rejected. It's just that—"

"Just forget it. Go to bed, then. A lot of women would love a kiss from me."

His words hit hard, and I hold my breath to avoid crying in front of him.

When I'm behind the closed door of my room, I lie down on my bed and press my face into my pillow so Henry won't hear my sobs. Despite his drunkenness, I'm miserable that he would speak such cruel words, and that he would bring up other women.

I sleep fitfully, and too soon, the sun rises. In a daze, I dress, moving around my room quietly so as to not wake Henry, and tiptoe to the front room to put on my coat and boots.

When I walk past the couch, I look down and see the pillow and the blanket neatly folded at one end, and Henry is nowhere to be seen.

Chapter 10

Thankfully it's a slow day at work, and not much is expected of me. Mr. Leung has me mopping the storeroom and wiping off the tops of dusty tins. It's a good thing I don't have to speak with many customers. My brain is clouded with a mixture of anger and hurt over how Henry treated me.

Halfway through the day, the bell dings as someone enters the store. I look to the front of the building and see Faye walking toward me. Faking a good mood is the last thing I want to do, but as she nears, I know I don't have a choice. I force a smile. "Hello, Faye. How are you?"

"I'm well. I haven't seen you for a time, so I thought I'd stop by and see how things are going."

"Things couldn't be better."

She nods. "That's wonderful. Are you free for a carriage ride tomorrow afternoon? I have to pick Charlie up in Royston."

"I'd love to, but unfortunately, I'll be working."

Mr. Leung overhears. "It's a slow day today, so I don't expect tomorrow to be any different. You may work a half day. It's okay."

Faye beams at him. "Thank you." Then turns toward me. "I'll pick you up when you're off tomorrow."

As much as I care about Faye, and as much as I'd love to spend time with her under normal circumstances, I'd love nothing better than to be left alone in my current state. However, I haven't a choice, so I keep a false smile on my face as I wave goodbye.

After work, I trudge slowly to the cabin, eyes on the path. A part of me still longs to see Henry, while another is disgusted by his behavior and wouldn't care if I never see him again.

As much as I've convinced myself he was wonderful, I didn't consider potential flaws. Drinking until drunkenness, in my book, is a big flaw. Choosing to drink over honouring our meeting is another.

I wish he had gone somewhere else last night. His neglecting to show up at the cabin entirely would have been much less painful. However, I realize perhaps it was a good thing he showed up in his condition. At least now I know how rude and hurtful he can be.

* * *

A low-lying blanket of grey covers the sky, making the air heavy and dank as I prepare tea before work. Stirring my cup, I walk to the window and gaze over the bay. Instead of the sea being a brilliant blue, it takes on the same drab colour as the sky.

I heave a sigh. It's hard to be motivated on an ugly day. All I want to do is curl up on my bed, forget about work, and, more importantly, forget about Henry.

After putting less than the normal effort into making myself presentable, I button my coat and make my way to the store, where I resume yesterday's task of cleaning cans in the storeroom.

Late in the morning, Mr. Leung interrupts my cleaning to inform me that he'll be taking his family to Vancouver in a week. "We will be away for three days. While we're gone, you will be the only one operating the store."

The thought makes my stomach churn. "But I don't know how to operate the cash register. And what if there are deliveries? I have no idea how to fill out the paperwork."

Mr. Leung smiles and reassures me that he will show me everything I need to know beforehand. His assurance, however, doesn't ease my anxiety. Wiping tins and stocking shelves is one thing, but running an entire store by myself is not something I'm in any way comfortable with the responsibility.

It's 1PM on the nose when Faye shows up with the carriage. I climb up and sit beside her, and she looks at me with a grin. "I'm glad you're coming along. It will be great to get caught up."

I smile back, desperately hiding my lack of enthusiasm.

On the way to Royston, Faye fills me in on the new things Eva is doing and how clever she's becoming. Then, she talks about the goings on in Union Bay, then asks if I've heard any news on the burglaries.

"Not really. I mostly keep my head down at work and don't pay much attention to what folks talk about."

"Well, you should take more notice, especially since you live near the beach. It's the homes and shops visible from the water that are getting hit."

"Yes. I suppose you're right." I sigh.

"You know, maybe you should consider getting a big dog. Intruders would think twice before approaching a residence with a protective dog."

"I don't think that's a good idea. I haven't learned to manage myself, let alone a big hairy creature."

Faye laughs, then points to the Royston store up ahead. "We're supposed to meet Charlie in front of the store. I'm going to hitch the horse outside, then go in and buy some saltwater taffy. I won't be long."

I smile as I remember Betty, and how she swore by the same treats from the same store.

Once Faye is inside the building, I leave the carriage and walk over to the small wharf, where I first met Henry. As I gaze down the long, narrow walkway, I see a small boat at the bottom, tied to the dock. It has a small motor off the stern and a large folded-up blanket inside. I return to the carriage just as Faye emerges from the store.

"We're a bit early. Do you want to walk for a while?"

I shrug, then follow her lead and stroll up the road beside her. She gives me a candy and tells me she and her family will be moving to Vancouver in a year.

I look at her in surprise. "What about Charlie's position managing the coke ovens in Union Bay?"

"I want Eva to be raised in Vancouver. The schools are much better. With Charlie's credentials, it won't be hard for him to secure a job there."

Even if I don't see Faye all the time, I always know she isn't far away. And even though Billy will eventually be with me again, I've gotten used to having her close.

Faye laughs. "I can see by the look on your face that I've caught you off guard. Don't worry. You'll be more than welcome to visit us anytime."

We hear voices ahead and soon come across a clearing filled with make-shift tents, wooden lean-tos, and people sitting on stumps, small stools, and turned-over buckets.

"What is this place?" I ask.

Faye looks somber. "It's a squatter's camp. A lot of these people are here because of the miner's strikes."

"But it's freezing at night. How do they manage?"

"I would guess the best way they know how."

My heart feels heavy as I take in the people and how dirty their clothes and faces are. There are a couple of fire pits with wire over them and open cans on top. Suddenly, I feel very guilty for having my two-bedroom cabin all to myself.

"We should head back to the store now," Faye says. "I can't see Charlie taking much longer."

We head back the way we came, and I don't say a word the whole way to the store. I'm too busy thinking about the poor souls squatting outside in the cold, trying to stay alive. A part of me wants to ask Faye about inviting some of the people to stay at my cabin, but I know she'd tell me it was too dangerous and that some of them could be troublemakers. If I held my ground and insisted on letting them stay, she might have Charlie move me out of the cabin and back in with them.

Charlie arrives in a buggy with other men dressed like him, in suits and overcoats.

Many of them have never needed to work a day at a labour job.

Faye gets into a deep conversation with Charlie and the other men. Feeling awkward, I walk over to the wharf. The same small skiff is still at the bottom of the dock, now filled with square packages and covered with the large white cloth I noticed earlier. Faye calls for me to come, and I return to the group.

In the carriage, we're just passing the dock when I look down and notice a man getting into the small boat. With a jolt, I recognize the brown hair and the way the man moves. It's Henry.

I immediately want to call out his name, but then I remember how horrible he was to me. Not to mention, Faye would find it in poor taste if I yelled out to a man she didn't know. I shudder to think how she would react if she knew that Henry had spent the night at my cabin.

* * *

At Faye's insistence, I have dinner at her place before Charlie takes me home. Walking down the pathway to the cabin, I ask Charlie his opinion about the homeless squatters. He tells me that as much as his heart goes out to them, he thinks the strike will end soon, and the men will have proper housing again.

When I ask him about the lack of food the people are enduring; he assures me that local restaurants and stores all give to the strikers, so even if they're without proper housing, they're not starving. I pray he's telling the truth, not just making me feel better.

As soon as I'm alone and in my cabin, my mind drifts from thinking about the squatter's camp to Henry. I know it was him on the wharf in Royston, but why was he there on that boat? And what was he transporting in it? Seems a little strange he would be on the water and not working on a construction site somewhere in the middle of the day.

Regardless, seeing him again did affect me. I wish it didn't, but it did. I thought he was a good guy who genuinely wanted to know me better, but after his spiteful words I don't think he cared about me at all. And now, with no hope of a relationship with Henry, I'll likely end up like one of those old spinsters living in small apartments in Vancouver.

You would always see them in the hallway, muttering to themselves and their cats! Why the heck do old spinster ladies collect so many damn cats?

I'm just getting up to boil water for tea when there's a soft knock on my door. Since Charlie only left a while ago, I presume it's him coming back to tell me something.

I put on a happy grin as I cross the floor and open the door.

To my shock, it's not Charlie on the stoop. It's Henry, standing in front of me with a sheepish expression. In one of his hands, he's holding something small wrapped in a red cloth.

"Henry. I didn't expect to see you."

"I know." His tone is soft and apologetic. "I've been a horrible person, and I wouldn't blame you if you never wanted to see me again."

I sigh deeply. "I don't know what to think. The last time we were together, you made me believe you were disgusted with me. To be honest, your behavior disgusted me too."

"Of course it did. I don't usually drink, and I can count the times I've been drunk on one hand. When I showed up here, I had been at the tavern with my crew. We had just worked a long day, and one of the men suggested we go for a quick drink. One thing led to another, and I lost track of time. The next thing I knew, I woke up on your sofa with a hangover. I was so embarrassed and left before you got up."

I study his face. "So, you don't usually drink?"

"I do have the odd glass, but it's very seldom. I never drink enough to lose control."

I can see in his eyes and how he keeps looking down that he is ashamed of his actions. And at least he's taking accountability for what he did. "Would you like to come in?"

He nods. "Very much."

We both sit on the couch. Henry holds out the item he's been clutching.

"This is for you."

"What is it?"

"You'll have to open it and see."

I gently take it from him, then unwrap the small red cloth. Inside is a box containing a pair of earrings with blue stones. I run my finger over the smooth stones, shocked. "They're beautiful. But they look expensive. You didn't have to buy them for me."

"I wanted to. And it was the least I could do after what happened."

He leans over and kisses me. Before I know it, we're kissing passionately in a tight embrace. My breath quickens, and my heart beats faster, and moments later, he picks me up and carries me to the bedroom.

* * *

I wake, my head rests on Henry's chest, and for a while, I listen to the rhythm of his heart and the slow pace of his breathing.

I'm so grateful he came here last night to clear things up between us. Otherwise, I would've thought he was an awful man with a drinking problem. Thankfully, I know better now. And now that he's taken my virginity, my feelings for him have greatly intensified. I know our relationship will only get stronger from here.

I could scream from the overwhelming excitement. I wish I could tell Faye about Henry, but I must approach the subject gently.

I lie motionless until Henry wakes. He smiles down at me, then kisses my lips. "Last night was your first time, wasn't it?"

I nod. "Yes. Of course."

"That is a gift I will always treasure."

I get up and make coffee while Henry gets dressed and then sits on the sofa. Once his coffee is ready, I set it in front of him on the coffee table, then sit beside him.

He picks up the cup and inhales its aroma. "Don't you have to go to work this morning?"

I sigh. "Soon. Unfortunately. But all I want to do is stay here with you."

"There'll be plenty of time for us. Plus, I also have work."

As Henry drinks his coffee, I suddenly remember spotting him on the dock. "You know, I saw you yesterday."

He looks quizzically at me. "What do you mean?"

"In Royston. You were standing beside a small boat loaded with cargo."

He shakes his head. "That wasn't me you saw, beautiful. It must've been some lucky devil that bears some resemblance." He chuckles.

"I could've sworn it was you."

"No, I'm afraid. I was nowhere near that area yesterday."

Soon, it's time to head our separate ways. Henry kisses me goodbye, then informs me that he most likely won't see me until tomorrow evening. I'm sad to know that I have a wait before seeing him again, but at least I have the memory of last night fresh in my mind to pass the time.

* * *

The day starts slow, with me cleaning out rodent traps and emptying trash in the outside bins. Thankfully, Charlie appears and breaks the monotony when he takes a few minutes to chat. He tells me Faye is home with a cold, so it's best to avoid visiting until she recovers. Then, he fills me in on the news about a burglary in Comox a couple of days ago. "Apparently, a lone man entered a store right beside the water. From what I heard, the criminal gained access to the building by boat."

"I can't believe that another place got hit. Did anyone see the burglar?"

"Sort of. An old man was looking out of his house window when he noticed a husky man in a dark cap carrying goods out the back of the store. When the old man yelled out, the burglar jumped in his boat and took off."

"That's terrible. What did he steal?"

"He got a pretty good bounty. A lot of food, money from the register, and some jewelry."

"Why haven't the police caught them yet? I just don't understand."

Charlie shrugs. "Whoever is burglarizing stores and homes knows what they're doing. They use the cover of night to conceal themselves, and in the daytime, they blend in with the rest of us."

"That's a scary thought."

"It's just my opinion. I may be completely wrong. But whatever the case, people are getting riled up at the police. They think more resources should be put in place to catch the burglars."

"And what do you think?"

Charlie shrugs again. "I think that luck eventually runs out. This outbreak of thefts will eventually end, probably sooner than later."

"Let's hope that's true."

Before Charlie leaves, I run back into the storeroom to grab the letter I wrote for Lou and Stewart, then ask Charlie if he wouldn't mind mailing it. He nods and tells me Faye will reach out when she feels better.

Later at home, I make a quick supper before changing into my nightclothes and turning in early. However, it's a long time before I can sleep. I'm kept awake by thoughts from last night and the romantic time I'd spent with Henry.

I can't wait until tomorrow. If he's here early enough, perhaps we can go for supper at the hotel. I'd love to be seen in public with him.

Then I imagine Faye catching wind of my romance before I can tell her. *Maybe going out in public isn't a good idea quite yet.*

Chapter 11

The clear skies of the morning are deceiving, as the day that follows is windy and cold. The day is slow at Leung's, and when it's finally over, I hurry home as fast as possible so I don't freeze. I'm thankful it's not a long walk when I finally latch the door behind me with numb fingers. I love living by the sea, but the lack of trees near the beach allows the elements to hit you with full force.

While making a sandwich, I open the cutlery drawer and spot a deck of playing cards that Charlie must have left for me. I grab the pack and set them down on the end table, thinking that maybe Henry and I can play a game together when he arrives.

However, the bad weather progresses over the next while, and I wonder if he'll show up. I sit back on the couch and play with the ring on my finger while strong winds gust against the windows and cause them to shudder.

I can't imagine how stormy the sea is right now. There must be huge swells in the strait. As much as I am aching to see Henry, I sure hope he's not on the water right now.

As time passes, I start to get sleepy. I am about to turn in when there's a knock on the door, and it opens before I even have a chance to get out of bed.

I stand up as Henry enters. He's soaking wet from top to bottom, and his skin looks stiff and cold. When he smiles, I notice that his lips are purple and shivering.

I quickly tell him to take a seat, then run to get a wool blanket. When I return, I sit beside him and wrap the blanket around his shoulders. "Are you crazy going out in this weather? You could catch your death."

He chuckles. "It's nothing. You're making too big of a fuss."

I go to the stove and put water on to boil, hoping a nice hot tea will help to warm him. Then I return to the couch and rub his hands between mine. "Tell me about your day."

"I had a great day. Do you know why?"

I shake my head.

"Because I had you on my mind from the moment I opened my eyes."

I giggle. "It was the same for me. I thought of you throughout my day as well."

After Henry warms up, we head to bed. All the tiredness I felt earlier subsides, and we make love through the night.

* * *

The weather stays in the same miserable mood for the next week. The strong winds litter the beach in front of the cabin with broken tree branches and debris. Yesterday, on my walk home from work, I found a small bird on the path. Its wing was broken, probably from being swept into a building or a tree. I carried it home inside my coat, but by the time I made it inside, the little creature had died.

In a short week, Henry and I have gotten closer than I ever could imagine. It's not often that he spends the whole night with me, but usually, every other evening, he stops in for as many hours as he can get away. When not immersed in passion, we're playing card games or just lying next to one another, talking. Every morning, I put on the earrings with the blue stones he gave me.

Mr. Leung and his family leave for Vancouver tomorrow. They meant to go sooner, but the bad weather caused a leak in their roof, and they had to wait until it was fixed. I'm not as nervous operating the store by myself as I was when Mr. Leung first asked me. Since then, he's shown me how to work the register and write up tabs for people who keep a charge account at the store.

I haven't seen any sign of Faye lately, or Charlie for that matter. Once I finish work tomorrow, I'll walk the long way home and stop off at their place to see how Faye is recovering. Hopefully, she's feeling better, and I can start revisiting her. I want to introduce her to the idea of me having a beau. Knowing Faye, she'll be skeptical at first. However, once she sees how happy I am, I'm sure she'll warm to the idea.

* * *

When I arrive at work, the Leungs are packed and ready to take the train to Nanaimo, then a steamboat to Vancouver. Mr. Leung passes me the keys, then shows me once more how to properly lock both the front and back doors of the store. Once they're gone, I do a quick check down the aisles to make sure everything is tidy and in place.

Tomorrow, I won't leave the main store area once we're open for business. I don't want one thing to go missing while I'm in charge.

As soon as I open the front door, three ladies walk in. Not far behind them is a couple of men. It figures—it's my first day alone here, and already it's busy.

Business snowballs and the foot traffic only slows when it's approaching closing time. My feet kill me from running to help customers look for items and then running back to work the till. When the last customer leaves, I finally pause, scan the entire store, and absorb the horrible shape of the aisles.

I nip into the storeroom to grab the broom, and once inside, I hear the bell chime. I must've forgotten to lock the front door. I quickly walk back into the main area of the store and see Henry standing at the front.

"Hello, beautiful. Perhaps you can help me—I am looking for a can of stewed tomatoes."

I giggle. "Oh, dear. I'm sorry, but we're closed. You'll have to come back tomorrow."

He hurries across the store, then sweeps me into his arms. "I am supposed to be working right now, but I had this overwhelming urge to kiss you." He presses his lips against mine.

It's just what I needed—a moment to escape from my hectic day and into the arms of Henry.

He then pulls back and looks around the store. "My, what a mess. Let me guess— you're the lucky one that gets to clean this place up?"

"Sadly, yes."

"I'll tell you what. If we move very quickly, I can probably spare twenty minutes or so and help you."

"You'd do that for me?"

"I'd do anything for you, beautiful."

As soon as we start moving, a competition sparks between us. Henry moves at lightning speed to straighten cans on the shelves and pick up scraps of paper on the floor. Meanwhile, I'm sweeping as fast as possibe. When I'm at the end of the last aisle, I see Henry standing behind the till.

"I never did understand how to operate these things."

I smile and walk over to him. "It's easy. All you do is push the amount of the purchase, then push the cash button, and the tray pops open." I demonstrate. "See?"

He laughs. "That was so easy. I feel like such a chump."

"Don't. I was intimidated by the register when I first started working here. Thankfully, Mr. Leung was very patient and didn't mind showing me over and over until I got it right."

When everything is in its proper place and the floors are nice and clean, Henry kisses me again and says he has something special for me that he'll bring to the cabin tomorrow night. My heart aches when he leaves the store, despite reminding myself that I'll see him in a day.

I focus on locking the doors to Mr. Leung's specifications. Once everything is as it should be, I leave the store and head over to Faye's. Charlie told me to wait for my cousin to reach out before I stopped by, but after days of no word from her, I feel more concerned. I know she's probably fine and Eva occupies her time, but I want to check on her to make sure.

* * *

As expected, when I knock on the door, Faye answers, looking chipper and healthy.

"Heather. How are you? I was going to get Charlie to stop in at the store to see you today, but he said he would be too busy. Come in."

After removing my boots, I walk into the living room to sit down, and Faye joins me.

"The last time I saw Charlie, he said you were sick. Are you feeling better now?"

"Yes. And it was nothing serious. Charlie tends to dramatize when he hears the slightest sniffle from the baby or me."

"Well, I'm glad you're okay."

"I am, thank you. But more importantly than that, I have some news for you. It's about Billy."

"What is it? Is he alright?"

She nods. "Yes. Charlie had to go to Cumberland earlier, and he went and checked in on your brother. He said he couldn't believe it. When he walked into the hospital room, Billy was sitting in a chair and speaking a mile a minute. The same as he's always done."

"You're kidding? That's wonderful!" Tears stream from my eyes. "Do you think he'll be able to be discharged soon?"

"I think that's a fair guess."

"I feel so badly that I haven't been able to visit with him since I started working. I hope he doesn't think I abandoned him."

"Don't be silly. Between Charlie and Stewart, Billy has been informed of everything going on with you. From what I gather, he's very proud of your progress so far."

"I feel so overjoyed right now. My brother is one tough guy. When I think about how tough of shape he was in after the accident, I can't imagine that he would recover so well in such a short time."

"Yes. From what I understand, Billy is a very lucky man."

I nod, then look around the room. "Where is Eva?"

"Sleeping, thank goodness. She's had so much energy lately that I almost need to nap when Charlie gets home to spell me off. But more importantly, what's new with you?"

I tell her work is going well and how I must be doing a good job because Mr. Leung left me in charge while he was away. I'm just about to start the explanation of Henry when Faye gets up to make tea. By the time she gets back to the living room with the hot drinks and a plate of biscuits, I've lost my nerve.

I'm sipping my tea when she looks closely at me and says, "My. Those earrings you're wearing are lovely. Where did you get them?"

Oh no. I'd forgotten I was wearing the earrings Henry gave me. Now that she's asked me, I can't lie. I'm going to have to tell her everything.

So much for easing into the subject.

"I, ah…I got them from someone. A man that I met a while back. When I was still living in Cumberland."

Faye sits up straight and stares at me. "Really? That's funny. You've not mentioned him until now."

"I know. I just wasn't sure where, if anywhere, our relationship was going. Now that I'm sure about him, I can tell you."

"You say he's from Cumberland?"

"No. I met him on the wharf in Royston while I was working for Betty's delivery service."

"And?"

"And, after our first meeting, there was something about him. Something different than other men I've met. Anyways, it wasn't until I moved here to Union Bay, working at Leung's grocery, that our relationship really picked up."

"What do you mean by 'picked up?'"

"Well, I mean that, um… I kind of fell in love with him."

She sets her teacup hard in the saucer. "How could you fall in love so quickly? Love doesn't happen that quickly, and you haven't been in Union Bay for that long. The only way you could have such strong feelings for someone you just met is if you were…" She trails off and gives me a long look. "Oh, no,

Heather. Please tell me that you haven't given yourself to this man."

I swallow hard and take a deep breath. "I...I really don't want to talk about this any longer."

Faye shakes her head. "Oh, no, Heather. Why did you give in to him? How old is he, anyway?" She sounds angry.

"I don't know. I never asked him. We don't focus on meaningless things like age."

Faye briefly puts her head in her hands and groans. "Take a guess."

"I don't know. I'd say he's probably somewhere around thirty."

"That's what I thought. He's probably thirty or older, and you are nineteen."

I'm getting increasingly annoyed. "Yes. So? What are you getting at?"

"He's over a decade older than you. Which means he's undoubtedly been around. At his age, he knows just what to say to get you to do what he wants."

"He's not like that, Faye. You don't know him!"

"Neither do you!" Faye lays a hand on my leg. "Heather, I care. I'm not trying to upset you. It's just that—"

"It's just that I'm an ignorant teenager easily manipulated. Is that what you think?"

"Of course not. I just know a bit about the desires of older men. I know how convincing they can be, and if you're not aware of that, you can find yourself over your head."

I can't believe she's this narrow-minded, especially when she's never even met Henry. I turn away, but then I feel her touch one of my earrings.

"Heather. These look expensive. What does your new friend do for a living?"

I sigh. "He owns his own construction company."

"Here in Union Bay?"

"Yes, Faye. His jobs are up and down the Island. And he's in such demand that he has employees working for him. That's why he could afford to buy me these earrings."

"I'm sure that's true. But I think I'll ask around about this man. There aren't many construction outfits in the area. It shouldn't take long to find out who he—"

I place my cup and saucer on the coffee table. "I'd best be going. It's getting dark, and I don't want to be walking home unable to see."

We both stand, and I thank her for the tea I never finished. She looks unhappy. "I can tell that you're annoyed with me, Heather. It would help if you didn't leave while you feel this way. We're family. I need for us to be close."

"I'm not upset with you," I lie. "As I said, I want to be home before it gets too dark."

Faye hugs me. "Can you come over again tomorrow? Maybe even stay for dinner?"

"Tomorrow? No. I can't come tomorrow. But maybe the day after." At this point, I will say anything to end this conversation and leave.

She looks relieved. "That would be lovely."

On the walk home, I'm seething and upset. Faye sees me as a mindless child. She proved that tonight. And why did I admit that I was no longer a virgin? How mortifying. As much as I love her, I wish like hell she'd stop acting like my mother.

She'd put a collar and a leash on me if she could.

My nerves have settled a bit by the time I reach the cabin. I'm ready to make a quick bite to eat, then go to bed. Other than the wonderful news about Billy and getting to see Henry, I've had better days.

* * *

Loud thumps on the front door rattle me out of sleep. Immediately, my heart lifts. Henry. He's found a way to come.

Excited, I wrap myself in a dressing gown as I hurry through the cabin to the front door, and I peek through the window to confirm what I already know. However, the person on the other side of the window isn't Henry. It's Charlie, and he has someone with him.

I slowly open the door and briefly see Charlie's smiling face until he steps out of the way and Billy stands right behind him.

"I can't believe it. It's you. You're here." Tears fill my eyes as I wrap my arms around my brother.

Both of us start to laugh as Billy squeezes me in his arms. "Hey, sis. How have you been?"

"I'm great now." I'm simultaneously laughing and crying. "I've missed you so much."

Charlie comes in for a few minutes, and the three of us sit around and talk. Billy says that due to the accident, he has some issues—the odd lapse in memory or smelling strange odors sometimes—but otherwise feels much the same as he did before.

When Charlie leaves, Billy and I stay up most of the night, getting caught up. He wants to know about my job, and if I've met any nice people since moving here. I tell him about the Leungs and how I can't wait for him to meet them. I even mention Henry to him vaguely.

Chapter 12

There's a strange wind blowing.

Staring out into the night, I watch the tips of the giant Douglas firs sway against the backdrop of the ominous black clouds. I feel uneasy, though I'm not sure why.

I look down at my forearms and see the fine hairs standing straight up. I close my eyes and breathe slowly and deeply, willing myself to calm down so the constricting feeling in my chest will ease.

It doesn't work. Instead, my mind speeds up as images of dangerous masked men breaking in and robbing the place flash before me.

I'm being ridiculous. I've got to stop my wild imagination before I'm driven mad.

I look around the store and force myself to concentrate on the tasks at hand. The floor still needs sweeping, and numerous items on the shelves could do with some straightening before I can call it a night and head home.

As I push the broom through the aisles, my anxiety starts to wane and finally draw a deep breath. By the time I'm finished sweeping, my body is limber, and my thoughts are turning at a normal pace, so much so that I feel ridiculous about allowing myself to get spooked.

After quickly straightening the cans on the shelves so all the labels point outward, I'm almost ready to put the broom and the dustpan away when I hear a strange scratching sound from the front door.

My anxiety spikes until I remind myself of the big Tom cat that often claws at the glass this time of night. I smile and shake my head, then go to the back room to grab my coat.

When I return to the grocery area, I turn off the main light switch to the building and am about to step towards the exit when my eyes catch a tall, shadowy figure quickly moving by the door. I stop in my tracks and try to focus in the darkness.

What the hell was that?

Knowing that the Tom cat couldn't have cast a reflection that big, I quickly realize that only a human could create a shadow that size and move that way.

The air escapes my lungs in one burst as though they were punctured. My fingers shake, and all the moisture in my mouth instantly vanishes. With my feet frozen in place and my eyes hyper-focused on the windows, a feeling of impending doom rushes over me. There have been far too many accounts of stores getting robbed around these parts. The fact that this store hasn't been hit yet is just dumb luck.

I look around the dark room, searching for something I can use as a weapon if someone does break in. Even though there's not much to me, I'm not about to go down without a fight.

Straining in the darkness, I can't spot anything I can use to protect myself, so I grab the only thing in arm's reach—the heavy flashlight sitting on the counter near the register. My hands shake so badly that I can barely point and turn the beam on.

Finally, I push the switch and a dull beam hits the floor. I slowly shine the light onto the windows, praying that I don't see a face looking in at me, but so far, I only make out the odd branch scraping against the glass.

No matter how terrifying it's going to be stepping out of the shop and into the darkness, I know I can't stay here all night. Billy will be worried if I don't make it home soon. I take small, slow steps toward the door, my chest only allowing short bursts of air to enter.

I'm only a few steps away from the shiny metal doorknob when the flashlight beam catches something pale through the window.

A face.

I gasp, and my entire body turns to jelly. I lose my grasp on the heavy flashlight, which crashes at my feet. The beam of light still points toward the door, and my eyes freeze in place.

Then, there's a flash of teeth as a grin spreads across the face on the other side of the glass. As terrified as I am, my body leans forward, closer to the person lurking outside the door. Then, I see a hand press against the window, and for the first time, I suck in a breath. The movement of the hand is familiar and non-threatening.

Then, the face makes sense. Distorted by the darkness, Henry comes into focus.

It's as though electric shocks run through my whole body. Slowly, strength re-enters my bones. I place my hand over my chest and exhale. It only takes me two long strides to reach the door and open it.

Henry stands in front of me with a wide smile. "Hey, beautiful. I wasn't sure anyone was in here until I saw the flashlight turn on. What took you so long to get to the door?"

I shake my head and let out a shaky laugh. "You just about scared the life out of me. I thought you were a robber."

"Nope. No robbers here. It sounds like your imagination ran away from you."

I nod, still holding a hand over my chest. "Yes. I suppose you're right. What are you doing here so late?"

"I was in the neighborhood and thought I'd stop by to see if I could walk you home."

I smile. "I appreciate that. Especially since I've worked myself up into such a nervous state."

Henry pulls me into him. I feel safe in his embrace as I rest my chin on his shoulder.

Then, just as I'm letting out a huge sigh of relief, two men appear in the doorway. Both wear handkerchiefs over the bottom half of their faces.

"Henry, look!"

Henry turns to the door, then quickly looks back at me. "I'm sorry, beautiful."

"What? I don't understand. What are you sorry for?—"

As I'm still talking, he reaches into his pocket and pulls out a dirty white rag. Then, with his free hand, he grabs the back of my head and stuffs the rag over my face.

An acrid odor of what smells like gasoline mixed with garlic burns my throat and nostrils. I struggle to breathe. Then, my vision narrows, and everything in front of me fades to black.

* * *

As I teeter on the edge of consciousness, anxiety rushes through me, and my heart knocks hard against the inside of my chest. Where am I?

All I hear is a loud humming sound. When I strain to open my eyes, there is only blackness. When I try to breathe deeply, I

215

choke on the suffocating stench of rotting meat.

It takes me a moment to identify the deafening buzzing noise as a symphony of frenzied flies. As soon as I try to lift my head off the hard dirt floor, a searing pain pierces behind my eyes.

Slowly, I reach out and feel the roughness of wooden slats as I run my fingers up a wall. Inch by inch, I maneuver my body until my back braces against the wood. Then, with whatever strength is left in me, I pound my fists against the slats and yell, my voice weak and raspy. "Help me. Please, get me out of here."

After a few terrifying moments of waiting for a reply and hearing nothing, I yell again, but this time I muster as much power from my lungs as possible. "Somebody, please, help me!"

The first creak I hear causes me to suck in full breaths of the rancid odour around me. Then, it happens again—the unmistakable sound of someone slowly walking across an old wood floor. Someone's coming.

I try to calm my breathing as my chest heaves rapidly up and down. I need to have my wits about me until I know what or whom I'm dealing with. I need to find out where I am and, more importantly, who brought me here. The last thing I remember is getting ready to leave Leung's store.

The steps grow louder as I rest my head against the wall and wait. I open my mouth to call out, but no sound escapes—my throat constricts with fear.

There's the unmistakeable sound of an old door handle creaking as it turns. I force air into my lungs and breathe out through my shivering lips. Disoriented in the darkness, I can only guess the direction of the noise. It isn't until dull light escapes through the opening door that I know which side of the room the person enters`.

Unable to make out any details, I stare at the broad silhouette. "Help me," I whimper, pushing myself forward onto my hands and knees, then slowly crawling toward the light. As I near the silent figure, something small and sharp, like a bone fragment or a chip of wood, pierces my knee and causes me to groan and stop moving.

The person finally speaks. "Where do you think you're travelling to, girl?"

"Why am I here?" My words are turning into sobs.

"Stay there."

I cry weakly on the floor as the figure exits the doorway, leaving only the dull light from what most likely is a reflection coming from a fire in a nearby room.

Soon, I hear the same sound of footsteps nearing, only faster. There's a much brighter glow coming from the doorway now, and I lift my head to see an oil lantern dangling above me.

I quickly glance behind me to see a bear cub carcass covered in a blanket of flies. I look back to the light just as it lowers.

"Heather. Are you feeling okay?"

The voice is familiar and deeper than the person that opened the door initially. It takes me a second to identify the voice. "Henry? Is that you?"

When he leans down and places the lamp in front of me, his grinning face comes into the light. "Hello, beautiful."

I force myself into a sitting position and look across at him. "What is going on? Where am I? And how did I get here?"

"Well, I'll let you come out of the room if you promise to behave. After that, I think you'll catch on pretty quickly as to where you are."

"Behave?"

Just then, a man appears in the doorway behind Henry. "What do you want me to do, Dutch?"

"Bring her." Henry stands and walks out of the room.

Bring her? But why won't he help me?

The man picks me up and drops me on my feet with one swoop. I wobble until he clutches one of my shoulders with a big hand and steadies me. Then, using the back of my neck as a handle, he steers me out of the room and down a short, illuminated hallway, to a small room with a rickety table sitting in front of a crumbling fireplace.

Henry is at the head of the table, emptying the remnants of a pipe into a tin can. Two other men are seated on either side of him. One is bulky and tall, whereas the other is frail and slender.

Henry motions to the remaining empty chair and orders me to sit. The brute loosens his grip on my neck and shoves me into the chair.

When I'm seated, I look across at Henry and the other men. "Where am I?"

The frail man laughs. "The same place we all are."

The rest of the men chuckle with amusement.

"Henry, what's going on? Tell me!"

I await reply as he takes out a small red pouch of tobacco and fills his pipe before running a match across the table and slowly lighting it. As he sucks on the long stem, his eyes meet mine. "You know what always irked me about you, Heather?"

Confused by his response, I slowly shake my head.

"You're a halfwit, plain and simple."

A sudden boom of laughter rings out in the room. I look around the table and shake my head. "Why are you speaking to me this way?"

Henry takes a long draw off his pipe and tilts his head. "I was hoping you would've been more of a challenge for me to catch. But instead of being a lion, you were more like a stupid goat—too easy to catch. You bore me. I could only stand being near you if I needed a place to cower down for the night and you were on your back."

Again, the room breaks out in laughter. Tears well in my eyes, and I do my best to conceal them. "You're a beast and a liar. And I bet your name isn't Henry, is it? I heard one of these men call you *Dutch*. You probably lied to me about everything, didn't you?"

There's a hush at the table as the men stare at Henry, waiting for his reply. The stillness in the room makes my hands tremble. It's evident he's the leader of the gang and more than likely the reason I was brought here and locked in that horrifying dark room. I'm quickly regretting what I said.

Henry slowly reaches into his pocket, pulls out a stained white rag, then tosses it onto the table before him. "Mind your tongue, beautiful, or you'll be taking another nap. One you may not wake from."

My eyes focus on the rag, and then I glance back at Henry—sharp images of being at the Leung's store flash through my mind. I see Henry after he walks into the store and him hugging me. I was so happy to see him.

Then, he pulls a rag out of his pocket, and men walk into the store behind him. I remember Henry pushing my face into the cloth and how I couldn't breathe. My head pounds as I struggle to remember more, but nothing comes.

With an amused expression, Henry watches me intently as I stare at the rag. He knows I remember something about what happened.

"You knocked me out, didn't you? Why did you do that? And why have you brought me here?"

Henry grins. "You know why."

I stare into his eyes as I slowly connect the pieces. "You robbed the store. That's why you were there so late. Only you thought I'd left already, and you knocked me out so I wouldn't put up a fight. Then, you brought me here—wherever *here* is."

As cool and as calm as can be, Henry nods his head. "Is that all?"

"Is Dutch short for Dutchman? As in the outlaw that's been robbing people up and down the coast?"

Henry smirks but says nothing.

"But I can't figure out your plans for me."

Henry takes a long draw of the pipe. The smoke swirls around his tongue, then slowly creeps out between his lips before disappearing into the air above the table. "I'm thinking of a reason to keep you alive. The way I see it, you're nothing more than a witness. An unwanted weight that will only slow us down."

My heart speeds up and my vision narrows. I start to hyperventilate. "My brother will be looking for me. In fact, I'm sure he's already gone to the police. By now, they're probably forming a search party for me. If you just let me go, I'll find my way home, and I promise to never breathe a word about you or your men."

All of a sudden, Henry stands up. Everyone at the table quickly leans back in their chairs, including me.

He turns to the brute who brought me to the table. "Charlie. Put her in my room." Then, he looks at the small, thin man. "And Bill, you take the first watch. I'll check on the boat, then get some shut-eye."

As Henry exits the room, I feel the thick hand tightly grasp my neck. "Move!" Charlie orders.

This time my legs feel less wobbly when I stand, and I can tell that whatever drug was used to knock me out is leaving my body.

Charlie steers me to the last room at the end of the hall. When he swings the door open, I see a cot on the floor below a small, half-opened window. The air here is still and reeks of sweat and stale smoke, but at least there are no flies or dead animals.

The brute shoves me into the room. I lose my balance and land on my knees as he shuts the door. I quickly scramble to my feet and wrap my arms around myself, then pace across the small floor.

How could I have been so stupid to fall for Henry's lies? And to think—all the while, he was the Flying Dutchman, robbing and pillaging shops and businesses up and down the coast.

It's like I've been thrust into some strange world where everything is unfamiliar and spinning out of control. I feel fragmented and confused. The only thing I am absolutely certain about is that I'm in real danger. I wish I were home with Billy in the safety of the cabin.

After hearing Henry talk about how I'm nothing more than a liability, a heavy cloud of impending doom hangs over me. If only I could see my brother again, I would hug him and tell him how much I respect and care about him. Mother would have been so proud of his attempts to make a better life for us after she passed.

I reach down to feel her ring on my finger, when I notice it missing for the first time since waking up. My heart sinks. *I hate you with every grain of my being, Henry.*

A door slamming up the hall startles me and adds to my uneasiness. Then, I hear Henry speaking to at least two of the other men. I quickly sprint to the door and press my ear against the thin wood.

The distinctive tone of Henry's voice travels down the hall. "I don't want any excess baggage. Tomorrow, take her out to the bush and put a bullet in her head."

A rush of terror races through me. I cover my mouth to stop from crying out.

"Why don't we just do it now?" one of the men asks. "It's dark as coal out there, and everyone here on Lasqueti Island will be sleeping. If they do hear a gunshot, they'll just assume someone had a bear near their property."

Henry chuckles. "Because I have a use for her tonight."

The men laugh along with him.

"Dutch, I've been thinking...I may have a purpose for the girl after all." The voice is meek and thin, which leads me to believe it's coming from Bill, the frail man.

Henry scoffs. "I can't wait to hear this. Out with it, Bill."

"Well, we have two more heists before we pack up and head south of the border. I was thinking that the lass could provide us with a diversion, so to speak."

"Bill. What the hell are you going on about?"

"Dutch, we could send her into these places before we strike at night. She could scope out where the registers and safety boxes are, so it saves us time when it's our turn. She ain't going to raise suspicion if she walks into a place, whereas one of us scruffy buggers might. Besides, I'm sure none of us want to be seen by a store owner where we could be identified later."

There's a long pause before one of the other men pipes up, "He's got a point there, Dutch. We can get rid of her after we do the jobs."

"I'll sleep on it. I'm going to bed. Don't disturb me. And Bill, you'd better do a good job keeping watch, or it won't be the broad's head on the chopper first."

Hearing his heavy footsteps approaching, I quietly shuffle across the floor to the other side of the room. When the door opens, the yellow glow from the lantern illuminates under his chin, casting shadows around his eyes and giving him an eerie, morbid appearance. Nothing about the man before me is Henry or who I believed him to be. This man is one hundred percent The Flying Dutchman.

When he walks into the room, a cold breeze enters with him. He doesn't acknowledge me. He passes by as if I'm not even in the room, then sits on the cot and sticks out one of his feet. "Pull my boots off."

The thought of touching him, this liar, this criminal, makes my skin crawl. Still, I know I have to cater to whatever he needs. If I don't, my stay of execution could be quickly revoked. I walk over to the cot, bend down, and grasp the heel of the first boot. Clumps of mud crumble off the leather and land on the floor.

When both boots are successfully set together next to the bed, I walk to the corner and prepare to sit when he looks at me and scoffs. "Where the hell do you think you're going? Get your ass over here."

My insides feel like glass shattering as I reluctantly return to the cot. When I stand in front of him, he grabs my hem and slams me down beside him, ripping my dress. In one motion, the monster pins me on my back and lurks over me like a starving wolf.

I close my eyes to blind myself from what will happen. My body may feel it, but at least I won't have images imprisoned in my mind.

"Open your eyes. Look at me."

I draw in a deep breath, then hold it. Slowly, I open my eyes and look up at the monster. His eyes are severe and focused, and the corners of his mouth are tilted upward in a sinister grin. *Please, Henry. Please don't hurt me too badly.*

I have been embroiled with this person before, but this time is different. He is no longer gentle and thoughtful. This version of Henry is aggressive and merciless as he yanks and manipulates my undergarments down my legs before throwing each piece to the floor. Naked and vulnerable, I do my best to keep my knees together, but it's useless. He pries my legs apart with one knee and slides his sweaty, filthy body against mine.

How could I have given my virginity to such a horrible man? What he said to his gang about me was right. I have been a fool, an idiot.

As Henry turns and twists my body in every position that satisfies his perverted desires, I think about being somewhere else, anywhere else. Like the beach in front of my cabin, watching the seals play just offshore. I think about Billy and Stewart and how much fun we all had at the Union Bay dance.

Then I think about what I said to Henry at the table, about my brother and the police looking for me. I wonder if Billy has contacted the police to launch a search party by now. He's still healing from his horrible accident, and I can't imagine him walking to the station to get help. Not yet alone, anyway. And then there's the possibility that he sloughs off my absence as something minor, like I had stayed at Faye's and forgot to tell him. The reports of criminal activity in the area have mostly involved burglaries, except for that one murder in Seattle. But never have I heard any talk of kidnappings. I'm sure Billy wouldn't equate my absence with anything so sinister.

After Henry—or the Dutchman—is satisfied and lying beside me, his mouth open and his chest heaving from exhaustion, my brain slowly becomes one with my body again, and I can feel every place he's touched me. I roll away from him onto my side.

As I lie on the damp cot, I can almost hear the pulse of my blood as it thumps and pushes relentlessly against the inside of my eyes. Nauseated from the pain, I use all my will to calm my body and keep from vomiting.

For the remainder of my darkest hours, I lie motionless until through the small, filthy window displays the first light of dawn.

I slowly sit up, careful not to disturb the man I will from hereon refer to as The Dutchman.

As I look out at the sun's orange glow, I feel like a different person. I do not feel dirty or used as I thought I would after last night. Nor do I feel emotional or scared. In fact, I feel surprisingly freed from all of that. I'm not sure why. Maybe the terror of thinking I was going to be killed and, afterward, the brutal way the Dutchman abused me, caused something to break inside. I don't know. Whatever the reason, all I feel is numb.

My head turns when there's a loud rap at the door, followed by a cautious male voice. "Dutch, we should be getting a move on the day. The sun is already up."

I glance down at the snorting body beside me as he throws an arm over his eyes. "Get the hell away from the door, or I'll put a bullet in ya. I'll be out when I'm damn well ready."

I look back to the window as the Dutchman twists and turns his body before sitting up and stretching. A wave of putrid, stale smoke, mixed with whatever remnants of alcohol he consumed last night, escapes his mouth and contaminates the air. "Get up and make me coffee, and whatever you can scratch up to eat."

"Are you sure you trust me to cook after what you did to me last night?"

His eyes follow me as I stand on the cot to step over him. Like the strike of a coiled snake, his hand lunges out and grabs my ankle. "I know you're stupid, but surely to hell you're not dumb enough to speak to me with contempt."

I glance down at where his hand clamps onto me. Then I look impassively into his eyes. "I may be stupid to you, Dutchman, but I'm not so dumb as to anger the person cooking my food."

I can tell I've caught him off guard with my snappy reply. He just stares at me for a moment, then releases the grip on my ankle.

* * *

Making breakfast for the gang of unkempt slobs proves a challenge. With only half a dozen eggs, stale cheese, and husks from hardened bread to use, I manage the best I can.

As soon as everyone finishes eating, Dutch stands up, and all follow suit but the waif, Bill. As Dutch walks past me and slaps my behind so hard it instantly burns, I grasp on tightly to the cast iron pan and imagine cracking him over the head until his brains spill out. But, knowing that act would be the last one, I quickly dash the idea out of my mind.

As I put on a pot of water to clean the dishes, Bill walks up beside me with a handful of plates. "Here ya go, Miss."

As I take the plates from him, our eyes briefly meet. It's funny, but without the others around, Bill looks like any old man you'd see walking through town, only dirtier. "I have a name. It's Heather."

Bill clears his throat in awkwardly, then repeats my name before turning and taking his seat back at the table.

"Where did the rest of your gang run off to?" I know they probably haven't gone far.

"They're fixing the boat. We've had some engine trouble."

"So, you've been left to babysit me?"

"It's really not like that, Miss—I mean, Heather. The truth is, I'm not very versed when it comes to mechanics. If I went along with them, I'd most likely be in the way."

"Oh, I'm sure you've got your strong points, Bill. Otherwise, Dutch wouldn't keep you around."

He nods, then starts fiddling with his thumbs, gently rapping them on the table. From everything I've seen of this man over the past few minutes, I can tell he's not only physically weaker than the rest but has a gentler disposition. This could be useful to me and better my chances of escape.

While the pot of water warms, I pull out the chair next to him and sit down. "So, Bill. How the heck did you ever get mixed up with such a motley crew? I can tell you are nothing like them. You seem more refined and wiser than the rest of your gang." I hope it's not obvious how I'm trying to build him up.

"Oh, I don't know about that, Heather. Dutch is far wiser than I'll ever be."

"Really?" I say, prompting him to divulge more. "I don't believe that. I can tell by the way you speak that you're intelligent. In fact, I bet if something happened to Dutch, you could run this whole show."

He shakes his head. "No. No, I couldn't. Dutch is great at masterminding. The rest of us just do what he says. So far, he's been right every time."

"Really?" I try to sound innocently excited. "What things has he been right about?"

Bill takes a moment, obviously contemplating if he should divulge whatever is on his mind. I reach out and touch his arm. "Don't worry, Bill. Whatever you say to me will stay with me. I'm just happy to have someone to talk to."

He shrugs. "I know what you mean. Nobody talks to me about anything unless they're ordering me around."

I shake my head with fake compassion. "That's a heck of a way to act to a member of their team. They should treat you with more respect."

"Yeah, I agree." He straightens his shoulders. "Especially since it was me who convinced Dutch to take them on."

"Take them on? You mean they weren't always with you and Dutch?"

"Nope. We didn't meet them until we left Butch Cassidy's gang in Wyoming."

I sit back in the chair and widen my eyes at him. "Are you telling me that you actually knew the real Butch Cassidy?"

Old Bill lifts his bony chin. "We didn't just know him. We were a part of his gang for a while and rode with him during his best years of committing train robberies and bank heists."

The more he speaks, the more it becomes apparent that he's not the sharpest tool in the shed. In fact, he's proving to be a real simpleton and a blabbermouth. Both of these characteristics can work in my favor.

I put a hand over my chest. "That's incredible. I almost feel like I'm sitting next to a famous person right now. I just can't believe you were a member of the notorious Cassidy gang."

I'm using my best theatrics. The truth is, I couldn't give a damn whom he rode with. Sure, I've heard of Butch Cassidy—who hasn't?—but by the looks of scrawny old Bill, I'm betting he wasn't a key player in the gang. At best, I see him charged with feeding the horses or tending the campfires.

"So, why did you leave such an exciting life back in Wyoming just to come up to the unforgiving elements of the North?"

"Oh, we didn't want to leave. One day, when Cassidy told Dutch and me to ride to the nearest town for supplies, we passed a large posse of lawmen in the hills. The both of us knew where they were heading—to find Cassidy. Sure enough, when the dust settled and we returned to camp, all we found were empty bullets and a couple of dead men on the ground. The law got every single one of them, except for Dutch and me. We got out of there just as fast as we could and didn't look back until we got to the ocean. From there, Dutch found a big boat, and we sailed up here."

"That's a very intriguing story, Bill. As soon as I saw you, I knew you weren't just an ordinary man."

He shakes his head, a somber look coming over his face. "But that's just it. I am just an ordinary fella. I mean, it's not like I didn't enjoy the train robberies and the heists. They filled me with a power I doubt I could explain. It's the killing I never had the heart for. The problem is, if you're in, you're in all the way. You can't pick and choose which parts you like best about being an outlaw. And Dutch, well, I'll just say this, he's

233

not the kind of man you want to oppose. If he says to do something, you do it, no arguing."

I shake my head slowly. "My goodness. I bet you've seen things only written in storybooks. You mentioned killings. I sure hope you weren't forced into shooting someone. That would be awful."

"I never killed anyone. As a matter of fact, I even tried to talk Dutch out of putting a bullet in that elderly man at the post office in Seattle. But he just pushed me out of the way and—"

The front door unlatches, and Dutch and the men walk in. When they reach the kitchen, I've already returned to the stove and am adding the dirty plates to the water.

Dutch looks quizzically at Bill. "What you two been up to?"

"Nothing, Dutch. Just sitting here, watching the girl, and waiting for you."

Dutch turns his eyes to me. "You two been having a good chat since we've been gone?"

"Are you kidding? That hopeless codger is as boring as old women at a knitting club. He wouldn't even tell me where to find a washrag. Next time, leave an animal to watch me. At least I'll have someone intelligent to talk to."

The gang, including Dutch, all burst into laughter, and I've provided an easy out for Bill and me.

Dutch tells me to leave the dishes, as he's got something he wants me for in private. I cringe when I see him turn and head down the hall toward the bedroom. I follow slowly behind him and into the room.

I have no idea what he's about to do or say. I only know for sure if he thinks overtaking me like he did last night will happen, he's in for a fight. I'll lose, no question about that, but I'll make sure I give him deep scars to remember me by.

I look at him warily. "What is it?"

"You're going to fix yourself up and look presentable. You're coming with us to scope out a place."

"And if I refuse?" My bold, sarcastic tone surprises even me.

He cocks his head sideways, then grasps my throat and squeezes hard. All air to my lungs shuts off, and blood pulsates in my temples.

"Don't get too brave with the attitude, my pretty little friend. Your fate relies solely on how nicely you treat me, and right now..."

He leans his face so close to mine I hear his teeth grinding as he talks.

"Right now, I'm feeling indifferent whether you live or die. Now, do as I say and get yourself cleaned up." He releases his grip, then walks out of the room.

I bend over, my mouth open wide to let in gasps of air, coughing painfully as my throat expands.

That sonofabitch!

As soon as I get my chance, I'll make sure his eyes are blackened out for good. *He may have broken something in me that can't be fixed, but I swear, as sure as I'm standing here, he will gravely regret the day he slithered into my life.*

* * *

The sea is choppy, and there's an icy wind rushing over the deck, chilling my bones. As the boat rounds the first bay, I look to the left, and off in the distance is a long stretch of land where dark smoke billows in plumes to the sky above.

It's Union Bay. It has to be. All that smoke must be coming from the coke ovens. My eyes strain to find my cabin on the beach, but we're too far away.

The boat veers to the right, and we head north. As we motor against the growing swells, Dutch yells over the wind to his henchman. I do my best to listen for every word as he tells them how tomorrow he wants all of them—besides Bill—to travel to the hideout in Seattle, where they'll all meet up after he hits the General Store in Union Bay once more.

Dutch senses that I'm eavesdropping and kicks the back of my leg. I quickly focus on the sea and step out of range of his feet.

As we head to God only knows where, I think about the Dutchman's plans for tomorrow. I wonder what he has in store for me if he intends to leave the area.

I'll need to stay vigilant like a hawk and wait for that one moment when he's not watching, not to make an escape but to seek my revenge.

* * *

The small bay is riddled with craggy rocks. Dutch instructs the largest of his men to take me to shore on the dory while the rest wait for our return.

Right before the oaf gets me into the small craft, Dutch grabs the top of my dress and pushes his face against my ear. "If you pull any stunt in there, I'm going to tear you apart like a wild dog."

I turn so our eyes meet. "Don't worry, Dutch. I'm stupid, remember? What stunts could I possibly come up with?"

Still gritting his teeth, he says, "Go into the store and ask about the postal services they have. While he's talking, look around for where the register is, and try to spot a location where they may keep a safe or a lockbox."

I grin. "Whatever you say, Dutch."

As the oaf lowers me into the little boat, Dutch keeps his eyes fixed on me. I get the feeling he suspects he may have

237

underestimated me or pushed me to my breaking point. Either way, I can't see him taking a chance and keeping me around for much longer. He doesn't want anything, or anyone, to get in the way of his big plans.

The ride to shore is challenging at best, with constant sprays of seawater breaching the sides of the small dory and drenching us. The large man says nothing as he lifts me off the boat, then points to a small wooden building at the top of the beach with a shop sign swaying in the wind over the entranceway.

It's a miserable hike across the logs and large stones. A couple of times while maneuvering over large logs, I slip and scrape my leg against the dead wood, earning me large painful slivers in my hands and shins. By the time I reach the building, I can feel blood trickling down my limbs.

Before entering the store, I turn and look at the brute on the beach, standing like a statue and fixated on my every move.

A kind-looking elderly man greets me as I walk into the store. "Good day, ma'am."

He looks me up and down, and I can almost see what he's thinking. *Who is this disheveled and filthy creature?* With a warm smile, he asks if there's something he can help me find.

"I'm new to these parts and thought I would come in and look around."

"I see. And where did you come from?"

"Wyoming, originally. Then, after a brief stop in Seattle, my husband and I just kept traveling north until we ended up here."

The man looks quizzically at me, obviously finding my story unusual.

I walk up to the counter and lean toward him with my hand extended. "I'm Heather."

The man shakes my hand and, as I hoped he would, continues asking questions. "Is your husband seeking employment in the area?"

I shake my head. "Not really. Dutch is more of a freelancer who waits for an opportunity to make money, then swoops in to make a quick profit. Dutch has always been that way, even back when I met him in Wyoming."

"Dutch is his name?"

I nod.

"I'll be sure to keep an eye open for him, so I can tell him we've met."

"Yes, you should keep an eye open for him. He's definitely one you won't forget meeting."

The man looks puzzled by my response but forces a polite grin. "You're awfully wet, ma'am. Can I get you a towel to dry yourself off?"

I shake my head. "No, that's okay. I should be going, anyway. My husband is waiting for me on the powerboat in the bay. But I'm glad I stopped in today. It was very nice to meet you."

"You take care, Heather. I look forward to seeing you again."

I turn and head for the door, then stop as soon as I grab the handle. "What time do you close every day?"

"Usually dinner time. Around five."

"Thank you." I exit the shelter of the store and re-enter the angry weather.

The ride back to the boat in the dory goes quickly. Too quickly. Moments ago, I was free...though, with the henchman standing close by. If I had run or tried to hide, things would've ended badly for me, and likely for the kind store clerk.

And even if I did successfully get away, the Dutchman would still be on the loose, free to commit his crimes and wreak havoc on innocent people. He's a master of evading the law, and I would never be truly free as long as he was.

No. That's not the way I want this story to end. If I'm to have any closure, I need to make sure he's stopped dead in his tracks.

On deck, Dutch corners me and glares deeply into my eyes, looking for any sign of betrayal. "What did you say while you were in the shop? And what information have you brought me? It had better be good. Your life depends on it."

"A large, young man worked behind the counter. He was unwelcoming and had a scowl on his face. I tried to engage in conversation, but he had no interest in talking."

Dutch hangs on every word. "And? What did you see inside?"

I shake my head. "Well, the first thing I noticed was a long shotgun resting in the corner behind a small register."

Dutch glances at his men, then back at me. "What else?"

"It was very strange in there. There was hardly any stock at all. I asked him why that was, and all he said was, 'We're closing down.'"

"Closing down?"

I shrug. "Yeah, I guess so. It doesn't really surprise me, considering how awful the man's personality was. He came off as an angry, defeated man with nothing to lose and a real chip on his shoulder."

Dutch tells the men to pull up the anchor, then declares, "We'll pass on this one and hit Union Bay tonight instead. We'll head back to the shack, gather our things, and get some shut-eye for a few hours. There's a long journey ahead of us."

Old Bill sheepishly asks Dutch what will be expected of him.

Dutch's brow furrows. "I told you already, you daft old man. You and I will hit the Union Bay Store, and the rest of the men will head south of the border to wait for us."

As we sail back to the dirty old shack, I replay my visit to the shop. I hope like hell I sparked enough concern in the old storekeeper to make him contact the authorities. I gave him every clue I could think of on short notice.

That being said, a lot of folks tend to mind their own business. But, even if he doesn't act on his suspicions regarding my strange behaviour, at least I deter Dutch from robbing his store.

With the gang scrambling around the shack, grabbing personal items, and getting ready to leave, I stand in the kitchen where Old Bill empties a small canvas sack. I watch bullets roll out of the bag and scatter across the table.

Then I notice a small, folded knife slip out of the sack.

I sit at the table and, while Bill looks over everything, I slowly reach out to where a bullet rests and flick it off the table. Bill curses when he hears the metal hit the floor and then bends over to pick it up. The moment he disappears under the table, I snatch up the folded knife and slip it quickly inside the neck of my dress.

As Bill resurfaces from retrieving the bullet, Dutch walks into the kitchen and orders me to wait in his room. As I walk down the hallway, I pray that the small knife doesn't slip past my waistband and fall noisily on the floor.

I sit on the edge of his cot and envision what my next move should be. With Dutch and his gang packing up and leaving the shack, I fear his use for me has run its course. He'll want to clean up any loose ends before he leaves the area, and I am, without a doubt, a loose end. I fantasize about different scenarios where, if executed properly, I could successfully end that monster's life.

He mentioned on the boat that he wanted to get some shut-eye before robbing the store tonight. If he doesn't have plans to get rid of me before he sleeps, the last chance I have to save my life and seek my revenge will be while he's napping.

I quickly maneuver the folded knife out of my dress and slide it under the corner of the cot. I finish using the edge of the blanket to conceal the weapon thoroughly when the door flies open and Dutch bursts into the room carrying a shotgun.

Chapter 13

Dutch watches my eyes widen at the sight of the weapon then walks over to where I'm sitting and points to the corner of the room. "Get off my bed."

I quickly maneuver across the floor and sit against the wall.

He lies on his side, puts his gun alongside him, and glares at me. "If you so much as move, I'll take this gun and blow your damn head all over the room."

As we lock eyes, a feeling of defeat washes over me. There's no way I can reach the knife even if he does fall asleep, not with the big gun he has nestled beside him. All hope seems lost to me now.

Our eyes remain on each other. I wait for what feels like a half hour, then slowly fake nodding off. I lower my lids until they're almost closed, then flip them open with a shake of my head as if I'm fighting to stay awake. The Dutch's eyes are on me the whole time.

It doesn't take long before I notice his lids getting heavy. They slowly close. A while later, his breathing deepens, and his lips fall open as he sucks in more air. He's sleeping.

Not knowing how long he plans to nap or if Old Bill is under instruction to wake him, I wait until I hear the guttural crackling of Dutch's snore before I make my move.

Slowly, I move from a sitting position onto my knees. Then, inch by inch, I slide each leg forward and closer to the cot. My hands shake as I slide them silently across the floor in front of me, and not once, not even for a second, do I take my eyes off the beast. My heart pounds so hard. I fear Dutch will hear it and wake to find me crawling toward him.

I'm almost there. Just a bit farther. I reach out to touch the blanket at the corner of the bed, but I'm not quite close enough. I crawl ahead again. This time, I will be close enough to retrieve the knife.

Just as I stretch out my arm, Dutch coughs, then flips quickly onto his back. Frozen with fear, I watch his eyelids, praying they don't spring open. *Please, please, let me grab the knife before he wakes.*

Knowing I might only have moments before discovery, I move until my fingertips touch the blanket. While watching him like a hawk, I quickly fiddle with the old fabric until I uncover the knife.

I pinch the weapon with two shaking fingers, then slowly pull my hand away from the cot. Once the knife is against my chest, I silently exhale and force new air in and out of my lungs.

Then comes the task of opening the folded knife. I have to look down to see if there's a trick or a button that does it. Every time I divert my eyes, I always expect to look back at Dutch and see open eyes and an evil grin. I continue pulling at the knife and searching for a way to release the blade, but nothing works.

When Dutch suddenly stirs again, I startle, and my shoulders pull back, nearly making me lose my grip on the small weapon. I grasp it tight and feel something on one side of the handle. I glance down and see a tiny silver button. I push down on it, which instantly releases the small blade inside.

I force in another deep breath to calm my nerves. Then, without knowing my plan, I clamp the blade in my teeth and slowly crawl beside the cot towards Dutch's head.

Once I'm kneeling beside him, inches away from his face, I look down at his exposed throat. I've never cut a person, or even butchered an animal before; this will be my first time. I fixate on his bulging Adam's apple and debate if I should stab above or below it. I decide to sink the blade into the divot at the base of his throat.

Feeling the pressure of time against me, I quickly position the weapon in my hand so the blade points downward, then raise the knife over my head. Then, I swing the knife down toward his neck with all of my might.

In that fraction of a moment, Dutch's eyes flip open. His hand springs up and grabs my arm, sending the small blade clanging across the floor.

No! No! No! This can't be happening.

Dutch laughs and sits up, still grasping my arm. "I was getting bored waiting for you to make your move. Now that you've failed, it's my turn."

I shake my head, not knowing what is going to happen to me but suspecting it will be terrible.

Dutch gets to his feet and pulls me up with him. Then he grabs my hair and runs at the wall, smacking my head into the hardwood. He lets out a maniacal laugh when I slide down the wall, dizzy and nauseous, blood pouring out my nostrils.

It takes everything I have to raise my eyes to him. I see the excitement on his face, like a predator pumped up on a kill. I slowly raise my hand to him as a plea to make him stop.

It doesn't work. I can feel the energy coming off him. He's just getting started.

I close my eyes and prepare myself as much as I can. I'm going to die in this dirty old shack by the hands of a madman. An image of my brother's face flashes through my mind, and I smile.

Dutch picks me up by the neck and, with enormous force, slams my head repeatedly into the unforgiving wall. With every impact, I struggle as hard as possible to stay conscious, but eventually the darkness overtakes me. As I'm drifting away, I hear loud banging on the bedroom door.

* * *

Thick pipe smoke burns my throat as my body shakes and shifts back and forth. I try to open my eyes, but they feel swollen shut.

It takes me a few moments to realize I'm getting carried over someone's shoulders. I attempt to move my hands, but they've been tied tightly behind me. My feet are tied as well.

The next thing I know, I'm thrown onto a hard, rocking surface. I know I must be on a small boat when I hear crashing waves.

I force my eyes open a sliver and see the millions of stars in the night sky. The boat jostles and I hear something placed on board. Then I hear Bill's voice close to my ear, "You just about didn't make it, Heather. If I didn't knock on that door when I did, he would've ended you right there. I got to talk quick so I don't get caught, but you got to pay close attention to what I say. Do you understand?"

248

I try to answer, but only strange groans leave my mouth.

"Dutch wanted to shoot you and leave you in the shack until I convinced him the other residents of Lasqueti Islands would find your body, and then there'd be no question as to who did it. So instead, he had me hog-tie you, and now he aims to throw you overboard on our way to Union Bay. I'm going to loosen the rope around your hands for when you are in the water. Hopefully, you manage to untie your feet. I'm so sorry about all of this, Heather. I hope you find the strength to make it."

I want to respond to Old Bill, but can't. I haven't the strength.

"What the hell are you doing, Bill?" Dutch hollers. "Get back to the shack. Grab the last sack of bullets, and don't forget the jug of water on the table."

The boat tips as Dutch gets on and Bill climbs off.

I keep my eyes closed as the stench of Dutch's pipe poisons the air around me. "Well, beautiful. It looks like it's almost the end of the line for you. Pretty soon, you'll be sucking in salt water and looking up as the surface grows farther and farther away." He chuckles.

A few moments later, I hear Bill return, out of breath. "I've got everything you told me to, Dutch."

"It's about bloody time. I chose the wrong man for my accomplice. I won't make that mistake again." The engines rumble under me, and then I smell the oily, thick smoke.

As the boat sways and pitches against the current, I think about how Dutch was probably right. With how weak and beaten my body is, I'm certain the last thing I'll see when I get thrown overboard will be the surface fading as I sink into the depths.

The ride goes fast. It seems like no time before the boat engines slow to an idle, and Dutch orders Bill to toss me over the side.

"Are you sure this is a good spot?" says Bill. "We're in the middle of the straight. There are always boats coming and going from Union Bay to the Islands. Wouldn't it be better to flip her over the side in one of the bays ahead? No one will spot her there, and with her arms and legs tied, she won't float for very long."

For a few tense moments, no one says a word. Then Dutch blurts out, "Fine! Whatever. Let's just get it done. The men are probably already waiting for us at the shack in Seattle."

Inside, I smile. *Thank you, Bill.*

Every once in a while, I force my eyes open to take another look at the magnificent stars, just in case it's the last time I see them. Before long, the engines slow again. But this time, I know Old Bill won't be able to give me any more leeway.

I feel Bill's boney hands grasp my arms as he pushes my body up and onto the ledge of the boat. Then he grabs my feet and, with one motion, flips me over the side.

The frigid water instantly sucks all the air out of my lungs, causing me to fight for every breath when I finally break the surface. True to his word, Bill did loosen the bonds on my wrists. I can jerk my hands free of the rope. But I am so weak, and my entire body throbs in pain. Still, I can't give up. I've got to try.

The water is dense and icy cold, making it almost impossible to bend my body so I can reach the rope around my feet. After numerous failed attempts, I decide to spend what little energy I have using my arms to slowly move forward. When the waves raise me up, I look toward shore and spot a small yellow light glowing on the beach.

I'm not far from there. If I could force enough sound out my mouth, someone could hear me.

My first attempt at creating noise is futile. A muted groan is the only sound that escapes. It's no use. There's no way I'll be saved out here in the darkness. No one can see me, and no one can hear me.

I barely finish the thought when I hear frantic barking from a dog. I wait until the swells raise my body and look at the shore again. I can still see the yellow light, but now there's a whitish-blue beam cast down the beach. It's a flashlight.

Someone is walking, and if I could only find a way to let them know I'm here, I'll have a chance at being saved.

I pull as much air into my tired lungs as I can. Then I open my mouth and give everything I have to make a noise, but once more, only a feeble mutter emerges.

Why am I even trying? I might as well concede to the fact that Dutch won. No matter how hard I tried, I couldn't beat him. I guess, sometimes, the bad guy wins.

The dog continues to bark as I slowly move my arms forward, losing energy with every stroke.

"What are you barking at, Red?" I hear a man's voice as if he were right before me.

Somehow, the dog knows I'm out here. But how? I haven't called out or made any noise. The only thing I've done is splash a little as I try to move forward.

That's it. He sees me splashing.

With the cold restricting my muscles, I can barely continue swimming, but I know all hope is lost if the dog loses interest.

I use every last bit of strength to raise my arms above my head, then slap the water in front of me. The dog immediately goes into a barky frenzy, and shortly thereafter, the bluish-white light shines directly on my face.

Sometimes I hear people talking around me, but I can't communicate. I don't recall being rescued, and I'm not sure if anything I've heard has been real or a part of my imagination. My eyes won't open, and I can't move any part of my body.

I'm sure I'm in a hospital because I remember hearing voices speak about my condition, using words like *coma* and *critical*. Faye came at least once but didn't do much other than cry. However, she did tell me a man named Luke Kingery and his dog Red rescued me. I smiled inside, remembering the time I met the kindly duo on the beach when I first moved to Union Bay.

I also remember hearing Billy's voice often as he sat beside me with his hand on mine. I remember him crying. He visited quite a few times, talking about how wonderful our future would be once I got better.

I also recall him telling me how the Flying Dutchman and his accomplice, Bill Julian, were caught after The Dutchman killed a police officer while robbing the Union Bay Store. He told me The Dutchman would hang but that Bill Julian got a lesser sentence in exchange for information about the notorious gang. Apparently, Bill told the law about everything, even about me. The last thing Billy said to me was that he got

Mom's ring back and now it's safely back on my finger.

The pain in my head has been growing fast and becoming more and more unbearable lately. I've given up on opening my eyes or moving my fingers or toes. It's too hard. The same can be said for my breathing. Every time I try to get air, it feels like another weight is added onto my chest.

As I often do, I fade back into the blackness, away from the noise and commotion. Only this time, when I return, my eyes miraculously open, and I can feel and hear everything. The room floods with warm beams from the morning sun, and all my pain has finally gone.

I take a long, full breath and sit up just as someone appears in the doorway—a beautiful woman with shoulder-length blond hair and the most beautiful smile I've ever seen. I rub my eyes to make sure the woman is real, and I'm not seeing things.

Sure enough, the woman is still there when I move my hands away from my face. Only now, she's walking toward me. The closer she gets, the more familiar she looks.

She reaches my bedside, and I can't believe my eyes. "Mom? Is it really you?"

She smiles and brushes my cheek, as she always did. "Hello, my angel."

I jump up out of bed and wrap my arms around her. "You look so beautiful. I've missed you so much."

She kisses my cheek, then gently takes my hand. "It's time to go now."

"Where are we going?"

"Home, sweetie. We're going home."

The End

If you enoyed this book, please leave a review. Thank you!

Also published by BWL Publishing Inc.

Hush
Shatter
Shiver
Storm
The Cove
Impulse
The Immoral
Deadly Ties
Run Baby Run
Snake Oil

2022 Bestselling Author

Jay Lang

Jay Lang grew up on the ocean, splitting her time between Read Island and Vancouver Island before moving to Vancouver to work as a TV, film, and commercial actress. Eventually, she left the industry for a quieter life on a live-a-board boat, where she worked as a clothing designer for rock bands. Five years later, she moved to Abbotsford to attend university. There, she fell in love with creative writing and wrote five novel manuscripts in a year. She spends her days hiking and drawing inspiration for her writing from nature.

BWL Publishing

bwlpublishing.ca